Pieces of Eight, Part III

Pieces of Eight, Part III

By
Jay Dubya

Bookstandpublishing.com

1972_4

ISBN 978-1-58909-310-2

Other Books by Jay Dubya

Black Leather and Blue Denim, A '50s Novel
The Great Teen Fruit War, A 1960' Novel
Frat' Brats, A '60s Novel
Ron Coyote, Man of La Mangia
Pieces of Eight
Pieces of Eight, Part II
Pieces of Eight, Part IV
Nine New Novellas
Nine New Novellas, Part II
Nine New Novellas, Part III
Nine New Novellas, Part IV
The Wholly Book of Genesis
The Wholly Book of Exodus
So Ya' Wanna' Be A Teacher
Mauled Maimed Mangled Mutilated Mythology
Fractured Frazzled Folk Fables & Fairy Farces
FFFF & FF, Part II
Thirteen Sick Tasteless Classics
Thirteen Sick Tasteless Classics, Part II
Thirteen Sick Tasteless Classics, Part III
Thirteen Sick Tasteless Classics, Part IV
One Baker's Dozen
Two Baker's Dozen
RAM: Random Articles and Manuscripts
Shakespeare: Slammed, Smeared, Savaged and Slaughtered
Shakespeare: S, S, S and S, Part II
Snake Eyes and Boxcars
Snake Eyes and Boxcars, Part II
Suite 16
O. Henry: Obscenely and Outrageously Obliterated

Young Adult Fantasy Novels

Pot of Gold
Enchanta
Space Bugs, Earth Invasion
The Eighteen Story Gingerbread House

Contents

Description

Pieces of Eight, Part III is a collection of eight unique short stories/novellas that complement the eight appearing in *Pieces of Eight* and the eight novellas represented in *Pieces of Eight, Part II and Pieces of Eight, Part IV*.

"An Attic Television" and "The Timeless Sports Car" are paranormal tales having '50s themes; whereas, "Time Vigilantes" and "Youth Revisited" lean more toward the science fiction side of popular literature.

"A Literary Dispute" and "The Better of Two Lives" mix elements of science fiction and paranormal experience. "The Hotel Delaware" and "The Rip Van Winkle Club" are essentially fantasy stories that incorporate science fiction and paranormal elements in their presentations.

"The Attic Television"

On *New Year's Eve*, December 31, 2001, John Peter Walker was celebrating his forty-eighth birthday with a bottle of his favorite scotch, *Johnny Walker Red*. The brand name of his most preferred whiskey had been chosen for consumption as equally by coincidence as it had by design. When on required business trips *Johnny Walker Red* was the introverted tycoon's most requested "on the rocks" drink in bars from Miami Beach to Honolulu. The tycoon was certainly addicted to that brand of whiskey.

John P. Walker was the richest man in Hammonton, and perhaps the wealthiest investor and entrepreneur in all of southern New Jersey. His good fortune all started with the acquisition of the family's road-paving materials' patent, which eventually led to lucrative contracts and enormous royalties from other area, national and international asphalt contractors. John's deceased father had acquired and owned the road sealant patent, but since the company founder had focused his energies on the day-to-day operations of his business the elder Walker never pursued the exclusive formula's economic potential. By 1990, John Peter Walker had taken over the firm and had amassed sufficient capital to finance a small army of equipment to honor major road-surfacing contracts all over the tri-state *Delaware Valley* region.

'Dad would have been mighty proud of my accomplishments,' Walker thought about his deceased benefactor as he liberally poured several ounces of premium scotch over a glass containing four ice cubes. 'I've parlayed my father's small paving business into a financial monster having no serious rival firms within a thirty-mile radius of Hammonton. It's too bad you and mom didn't live to see *my* great success,' John P. Walker lamented as he raised his glass to his lips, respectfully saluting an oil portrait of his deceased parents on the mansion's den wall. Then the highway-paving mogul slowly sipped the rich whiskey, savoring its unique taste. 'Yes Dad and Mom,' the young man sincerely acknowledged, 'I'm grateful for my inheritance and I promise I'll be diligently pursuing the company's excellent reputation until the day I die!'

A rapping at the walnut-paneled den's door was followed by the entrance of Giles pulling a handle and Hillary pushing the rear of a metal squeaky-wheeled cart having an ancient table-model television on its top.

"Where should we leave it Mr. John?" Giles Wood, Walker's faithful butler politely asked his rather eccentric and presently apathetic employer.

"Next to that far wall near the electrical socket," Walker pointed and answered rather imperatively. "Right in front of that shelf of rare books."

"Don't tell me Sir that you plan on watching this old rather obsolete contraption?" Hillary Wood, the loyal Walker' maid jested. "This thing is as old as *you* are. In fact, it *is* exactly as old as you are!"

"You don't say," John P. Walker replied. "Then that bulky museum piece would've had to be manufactured in or around the remarkable year 1954," he added realizing the unique parallel.

"That is correct," Giles affirmed with absolute certainty. "It was manufactured the same year *you* were born, exactly forty-eight years ago. What a curious coincidence! But I'm afraid that this antique has seen better days."

"They don't make *Emersons* any more," Walker seriously interrupted. "If I recall from my childhood this particular unit was one of the company's most popular items. It has a twenty-one inch bowed screen with a control panel on the left," the mansion owner recollected and related. "And I still vividly remember this relic from when I was a kid sitting on my Daddy's knee. My God Giles and Hillary, time' marches on, doesn't it?"

"Many brand names have gone out of business since then in the television market," Giles recollected and mentioned. "Besides *Emerson*, I remember TV sets with extinct names like *Muntz, Philco, DuMont* and *Admiral*. Those TV products have all gone the way of the *Edsel, the Hudson* and the *Packard* in the post *World War II* automobile industry."

The very wealthy man contemplated his fleet of thirteen classic cars parked in a huge garage recently added onto his impressive mansion, one of which was a mint-condition '54 brown *Packard*. His reverie was interrupted as the conversation continued.

"And Mr. Walker," the maid courteously stated, "it was very kind of you to donate this exquisite *Emerson* television to the Hammonton Historical Society Museum. It's indeed a real collectors' item," Hillary Wood continued, "and it was only gathering a pound of dust up in the attic. My husband and I thoroughly cleaned it up from top to bottom before we carefully transported it to your den."

"That will be all for now," John P. Walker thanked his servants before gulping down another mouthful of his favorite scotch. "Giles and I will take it over to the historical society on Wednesday. Tomorrow's *New Year's Day* and I guarantee you no one will be there to accept this noteworthy treasure from the '50s. Giles," Walker continued, "do you remember us watching shows like *Ed Sullivan, Jackie Gleason, Milton Berle, Jack Benny* and *I Love Lucy* on this splendid device?"

"I most certainly do Sir," the straight-laced butler recalled, "and if my failing memory serves me correctly, we also had viewed many episodes of *Howdy Doody, Dragnet, The Life of Riley* and *Ozzie and Harriet* too."

"*Ozzie and Harriet*," Walker indulgently laughed. "The perfect '50s American family. If only life today was as simple and laid back as it had been back in the nifty fifties. Of course," the multimillionaire continued prattling, "I've become filthy rich over the last dozen years," the road-paving baron boasted, "so I guess I can trade a little complicated existence and aggravation for a modern huge bank account. In the final analysis," Mr. John Peter Walker assessed, "the prospect of a prosperous and profitable 2002 doesn't seem that bad after all. Cheers to the *New Year*!" the wealthy fellow said as he lifted his glass.

"Anything you say Mr. Walker," Giles amiably agreed. "You must be a very intelligent man since you've made many clever strategic money decisions to expand the family' business in the last decade."

"Actually, my decisions involved more luck than intellect," Walker reluctantly admitted to his butler and maid. "It was more like being in the right place at the right time than anything else. But I want to thank you both for finding and bringing in this archeological artifact," the happy resident related. "Stop by after midnight and we'll celebrate the *New Year* by polishing-off the remainder of this fine bottle of scotch. See you both in about an hour right before the grandfather clock' chimes strike twelve. And Giles," Walker said with a smile, "don't forget to grease those squeaky wheels on that metal cart."

"Thank you Sir and I promise you I won't forget," Giles pleasantly answered. Then the butler and his accommodating wife jointly exited the luxurious den.

John P. Walker was a self-confirmed recluse. He shied away from having close friends, thinking that they would be more interested in his prolific *Merrill Lynch Cash Management Account* than in the distrustful man's true companionship. There were hundreds of acquaintances in his computer e-mail address book, but his dependable friends could be counted twice on a thumb-less hand. 'A secret is only a secret when it belongs to me,' the slightly paranoid man reckoned. 'As soon as it is shared with one other person it's a secret in jeopardy.'

The self-made businessman poured another glass of delicious scotch and sat back on his cranberry-colored soft leather sofa. 'Materialism is great,' he thought. John P. Walker was tempted to grab his remote control and activate his large-screen television featuring stereo sound, but suddenly the middle-age gentleman felt a temptation to get up and casually saunter over to the early '50s *Emerson* set that was still situated on top of the squeaky-wheeled metal cart.

Then Walker chuckled as he had an inspiration. 'I'm going to plug this baby in to see if I could get more than static on the screen,' he laughed, placing his scotch drink on the convenient TV cabinet. 'I wonder if this antiquated thing still conducts electricity after sitting idle up in the attic for over forty years. I suppose I'll soon find that out!'

John P. Walker reached around the set and soon found the device's electric plug. Then he inserted the two-pronged object into the wall socket, meticulously turned the "ON/OFF" knob in the control panel, adjusted the "rabbit ears" and impatiently waited to see if anything would happen.

In ten seconds the vintage *Emerson* TV's picture tube illuminated. John rotated the station selector to 1, noticing that the old set had thirteen channels on its dial. To Walker's delight and amazement, a news broadcaster appeared on the black and white picture tube. The mildly astonished man increased the set's volume on the control panel, lifted his scotch on the rocks from the top of the television cabinet and then returned to his soft cranberry-leather' sofa.

"Why that's Douglas Edwards sitting behind a studio desk doing his nightly news program!" John P. Walker marveled and uttered. "This must be a '50s television rerun special or something," he theorized and softly expressed. "That news show went off the air maybe thirty-five years ago, and Douglas Edwards is certainly now deader than a doornail, no doubt about it. Gee, nostalgia is a wonderful thing!" he said to no one but himself'. "Let's see what good old deceased Douglas Edwards has to report."

"In January news," Douglas Edwards began, "the highly motivated Michigan State Spartans defeated the UCLA Bruins in the annual *Rose Bowl Game* by a score of 28-10. The football extravaganza was played before a capacity crowd in Pasadena, California. Now moving on to some favorable economic news," Douglas Edwards said and paused as his hands shuffled to the next page, "*General Motors* has announced that the giant corporation is planning a one billion dollar retooling and expansion to its popular line of automobiles, which includes *Chevrolet, Pontiac, Oldsmobile, Buick* and *Cadillac*. In other jobs-related news," the serious-faced Douglas Edwards remarked, "on January 19th, the Senate will approve construction of the *St. Lawrence Seaway*. The new project is designed to…"

John P. Walker reckoned he would step to the fascinating television set and perform an experiment by manually changing the channel. Returning to his soft leather sofa, the successful entrepreneur was more than surprised to notice that Douglas Edwards was also doing the news on Channel 2 as he had been presenting on Channel 1. Walker could not believe his eyes and his ears upon contemplating the bizarre phenomenon. The wealthy fellow settled into his comfortable seat, poured another measure of *Johnny Walker Red* onto the shrunken ice cubes in his glass, and started to imbibe more of the potent alcohol as he scrutinized the black and white TV screen.

"On February 2nd of this year President Eisenhower officially disclosed for the record that the first hydrogen bomb had been detonated back in 1952 at Eniwetok Atoll in the Pacific," Douglas Edwards reported. "The bomb was extremely powerful, according to sources, and it…"

John P. Walker had again risen from the sofa and changed back to Channel 1 to test a theory that was swimming around in his half-intoxicated mind. The results of his effort proved rather disconcerting to his sense of rationality because the Douglas Edwards broadcast was still in progress.

"In a special message to Congress," Douglas Edwards read from his teleprompter, which apparently was now functioning properly, "President Eisenhower today urged widespread modifications to the much-maligned Taft-Hartley labor law. It should be noted that our chief executive has staunchly advocated a return to flexible farm price supports."

The bewildered viewer switched back to Channel 2. Douglas Edwards was calmly reporting another pertinent event to his faithful American audience. "On February 23rd, Dr. Jonas Salk, the developer of a breakthrough serum against polio, administered injections of the vaccine to Pittsburgh school children. The inoculations are scheduled to continue for the remainder of the month and then the results will be evaluated throughout the course of the year," the news sole anchorman disclosed. "And now on the entertainment scene, *The Confidential Clerk,* a popular play by celebrated writer T.S. Eliot opened at New York City's Morosco Theater. The new *Broadway* production stars Claude Rains and Ina Claire as…"

'This is absolutely incredible!' John P. Walker imagined. 'Each channel seems to correspond to a different month in 1954. Channel 1 was January and Channel 2 is February. If my crazy theory is correct, Channel 3 will be March.' The man's head was dizzy from the shock of his observation and from the accumulative potency of the scotch whiskey.

Sure enough, Channel 3 was featuring the March 1954 news, so John P. Walker tried twisting his neck first left and then right to shake out the loose cobwebs and to sober up a bit. Being intrigued by the surreal mystery his eyes and mind had been interpreting, the extremely puzzled fellow returned to the comfort of his fine leather sofa.

"On March 1st," Douglas Edwards professionally indicated, "five Congressmen were shot by Puerto Rican Nationalists on the floor of the *House of Representatives.* All five are recovering from their gunshot wounds. In sports," Edwards conveyed, "Tom Gola led the *LaSalle Explorers* of Philadelphia to the NCAA Basketball Championship in a spectacular and impressive 92-76 win over *Bradley.* And on March 25th," the broadcaster continued in his standard monotone voice, "an *Academy Award* was presented to *From Here to Eternity* as the best motion picture of 1953 and an *Oscar* was earned by William Holden for his best actor performance in *Stalag 17.* Switching back to domestic and

6

international events," the news' personality very deliberately proceeded, "on March 25th President Eisenhower revealed that a hydrogen bomb explosion in the Marshall Islands had exceeded all military estimates and government expectations. The blast definitively proved that the United States is ahead of Russia in the nuclear arms research and development race."

Being absolutely captivated with what his' mind was processing John P. Walker again stepped to the very extraordinary *Emerson* television and abruptly twisted the selector dial to Channel 4. The perplexed man poured another few ounces of *Johnny Walker* and mechanically chugged the whiskey down the hatch. 'Douglas Edwards was on the air even before Walter Cronkite!' Walker marveled and evaluated. 'This whole thing is some sort of exceptional paranormal experience. It's too fantastic to be a clever prank or a practical joke!'

"On April 16th," Douglas Edwards announced with a stoic expression on his familiar countenance, "the *Detroit Red Wings* defeated the *Montreal Canadiens* in the Stanley Cup finals, four games to three. *Motor City* ice hockey fans celebrated the team's victory by…"

John Walker had again risen from his soft leather sofa and aggressively flicked the dial to the left back to Channel 3 to determine if the March of '54 news was still in progress. "On March 10th," Douglas Edwards said, "federal officials divulged that the Atomic Energy Commission approved plans for the *Duquesne Power Company* of Pittsburgh to construct the first nuclear power electric generating plant. The new facility is scheduled to go from drawing board to…"

The now-inebriated viewer hastily flicked the channel rotator forward from position three to four, or from March to April. John P. Walker staggered back to his seat very confounded by what his normally reliable five senses had been receiving and the astounded viewer was quite perplexed by what his' confused mind had been comprehending and reviewing. His common sense told him to deny all that was being perceived.

"Congress has authorized the construction of the *United States Air Force Academy*," Douglas Edwards confidently reported, "and it will be a first class institution that will rival similar military academies at West Point and at Annapolis. The site of the new school will be somewhere in Colorado, but the exact location will not be made public by the federal government until two months from now in early June."

The now-drunk and annoyed tycoon got up and switched to Channel 5 and then slowly trudged back to his comfortable leather den sofa. He incredulously glanced at his quart bottle of *Johnny Walker Red*, which was now only half' full. The peeved and neurotic observer once again plopped down into the soft center cushion of his cranberry-colored sofa. The fellow again reached over and filled his glass with whiskey and then blankly stared at the classic television situated directly before his eyes.

Douglas Edwards was peering into the camera at his loyal 1954 nightly television audience. "The big news in May is that the U.S. Supreme Court in a landmark decision declared that racial segregation is unconstitutional in the nation's public schools. The practice of 'separate but equal', prevalent mostly in the American South up to the present time, will no longer be a viable argument to prevent the creation of racial integration into our nation's public schools." The famous anchorman cleared his throat and continued with his long-winded recitation. "Most of you viewers already know that the 80th running of the *Kentucky Derby* was won by *Determine* in a time of two minutes and three seconds. Jockey Ray York was aboard the victorious thoroughbred as it triumphantly made its way to the *Churchill Downs* Winner's Circle. *Determine* will now attempt to achieve horse racing's most coveted honor, the *Triple Crown*. The next difficult challenge after the *Derby* will be the *Preakness,* which later in June will be followed by the ever-popular *Belmont Stakes*."

Wholly intoxicated, John P. Walker awkwardly stood and clumsily approached the ancient electronic mechanism. The annoyed gentleman anxiously turned the selector to Channel 6. "Well now I'll review some more ancient history," he stated to himself. "It all seemed so damned important back in 1954 but now it all seems so terribly haunting, so ugly and eerie. I always suspected that Douglas Edwards was a charlatan back when I was a kid. Now I realize the idiot must be an evil sorcerer. What on earth has happened to sanity?"

The befuddled asphalt merchant slowly shuffled back to his familiar soft leather sofa. He instinctively imbibed another mouthful of scotch as the 1954 June news appeared on the *Emerson* television screen.

"According to *Air Force* Secretary Harold E. Talbott," Douglas Edwards aptly stated, "the site of the new highly anticipated *Air Force Academy* will be Colorado Springs, Colorado. Elated government official gathered today, June 6th to officially make the announcement before…"

John P. Walker predictably rose and rushed to the fifties' table-model television perched on top of the metal cart. He roughly rotated the knob counterclockwise to May. On Channel 5, Douglas Edwards blandly declared, "The 38th *Memorial Day Indianapolis 500 Auto Race* was won by Bill Vukovich, who achieved an admirable average speed of 130.8 miles per hour. It was Vukovich's second consecutive *Indy'* triumph. Congratulations Bill! And now on to some regular news."

The groggy' viewer still standing in front of the *Emerson* shook his head in total disbelief. A puzzled look remained on his face and his fingers gripped and advanced the dial ahead to Channel 7 to review some of July's relevant events. Walker slowly sipped his glass without ever thinking about adding fresh ice cubes, which had all partially melted inside of an opened metal ice bucket disguised as a knight's helmet. In disgust, Walker slammed the ice bucket's knight visor shut.

Douglas Edwards' grim face and penetrating eyes nearly filled the black and white television screen and presently occupied the attention of its somewhat hypnotized viewer.

"The '50s were a time of black and white," Walker mumbled and maintained to himself'. "Sneakers were black and white, television screens were black and white, camera pictures were black and white, newspapers were black and white and segregation was black and white. What the hell is going on here? Devil, show yourself!"

"On July 13th," the stern-faced news commentator prefaced, "the Gross National Product for 1953 was officially announced. The Department of Commerce indicated that the *GNP* was put at 365 billion dollars and that this hefty statistic illustrates the prosperity of a growing and thriving American economic system. On the sports scene," the highly rated announcer read from his teleprompter, "the world tennis championships at *Wimbledon* are scheduled to resume today in merry old England. Vic Seixas and Maureen Connally are the men's and women's' favorites respectively. The annual tournament is a highlight of each summer, and participants are honored to enthusiastically compete in the prestigious classic each..."

The disbelieving viewer again habitually rose from his comfortable sofa and stubbornly twisted his wrist to the left back to Channel 6. "The June calendar is highlighted by the annual running of the *Belmont Stakes*," Douglas Edwards matter-of-factly articulated, "and *High Gun* won the highly-contested event with jockey Eric Guerin proudly escorting his champion steed to the Winner's Circle. *High Gun* won the racing contest with an impressive time of two minutes and..."

John P. Walker desperately switched ahead to Channel 8 to investigate into 1954 August news. The addled viewer's patience and prudence were eroding as rapidly as his sobriety. He stood slumped over, leaning against the metal cart that held the now despicable obnoxious-sounding heirloom *Emerson* table-model television.

"On August 9th," the famous news broadcaster asserted, "Cooperstown's *Baseball Hall of Fame* inducted nine new members. Topping the list of new inductees was..."

Walker disgustedly and vigorously changed the station to Channel 9. He dejectedly reentered his spot on the still comfortable leather sofa and sank down into the cranberry-dyed central cushion. His heart, mind and soul were in a total quandary. 'This whole damned thing reeks of evil,' Walker thought, 'and I don't have the will or the strength to fight it. I'm a hapless victim and nothing more,' the man concluded as he swallowed down another quantity of scotch.

"Back on September 6th Vic Seixas and Doris Hart respectively had won the men's and women's' divisions *of The U.S. Lawn Tennis Association Tournament*," Douglas Edwards reported and reminded the nation's viewers on Channel 9. "And today September 24, the *United Steel Workers of America* banned all communists, fascists and card-carrying members of the *Ku Klux Klan* from its ranks. In other national news," the commentator competently continued, "the *U.S.S. Nautilus*, the first atomic powered submarine' is slated to be commissioned at Groton, Connecticut. On hand for the momentous occasion will be..."

John P. Walker had just enough strength to wobble across the palatial den to the *Emerson* table-model television and savagely advance the selector to Channel 10. He leaned against the metal cart to support his almost limp anatomy with his left hand while holding his half-full glass of scotch with his right.

"Our news department has recently learned that on October 13th, the much-heralded B-58, our nation's first supersonic bomber was ordered into production by the *Air Force*," the commentator said. "And yesterday, October 15th, *Hurricane Hazel* ravaged the eastern coastline causing widespread devastation and loss of life. The most violent hurricane in decades has killed ninety-nine persons in the U.S. and another two hundred and forty-nine in Canada. Combined North American property losses are estimated at over a hundred million dollars," Douglas Edwards glibly disclosed. "And finally, in the dynamic publishing world, the literary community is looking forward to this year's *Nobel Prize for Literature.* The leading candidate for the coveted award is reputed to be Ernest Hemingway, whose most renown literary contributions were the novels *The Sun Also Rises, A Farewell to Arms* and *For Whom the Bell Tolls.* The announcement will be made October 28th at the *Nobel Prize* headquarters in…"

The now totally drunken American "new money aristocrat" stooped down and rotated the channel dial one notch to the right. "I still remember that damned destructive *Hurricane Hazel*," he muttered to his scotch glass. "It blew the roof off of almost every flimsy house in the Hammonton area. And that overrated author Hemingway was nothing more than a mentally sick perverted alcoholic."

"In the November 2nd national elections," Douglas Edwards austerely articulated, "the Democrats gained a valuable additional seat in the *Senate* for a narrow but important 48-47 majority over the Republicans. In the *House of Representatives,* Democrats gained twenty-one seats to establish a 232-203 majority. President Eisenhower expressed his disappointment at the outcome of this year's…."

"Who cares about damned 1954 politics?" John P. Walker exclaimed. "It's as dumb an activity as religion is, and both subjects are unworthy of public discussion or debate," the inebriated man mumbled as he emphatically twisted the television knob to the left back to Channel 10. "I already know what happened in 1954," the rich man mumbled and complained, slurring his words.

"The fifty-first *World Series'* best of seven games was decisively won in a surprising four games to none victory by the *New York Giants*, who easily vanquished the favored *American League Cleveland Indians* despite Cleveland's supposedly superior pitching staff consisting of veterans Bob Feller, Mike Garcia, Early Wynne and Bob..."

The road paving *CEO* managed to regain his equilibrium, traipse to the aforementioned television and switch the selector ahead to Channel 11, where the November 1954 news was still being delivered. Walker gawked down at the television set with his mouth agape.

"Yesterday November 4th," Douglas Edwards very formally announced, "the much-acclaimed musical *Fanny* opened on *Broadway*. S. N. Behrman and Joshua Logan have written the show, which is expected to draw..."

Realizing that the ongoing phenomenon he' was witnessing had been verified by checking and re-checking the monthly events on various channels, John P. Walker rotated the television knob to Channel 12. The now apprehensive skeptic retreated to his soft cranberry-colored leather sofa and with a trembling hand poured the remaining contents of the *Johnny Walker Red* bottle into his ice-less crystal glass.

"Now it's finally December of '54," the asphalt contractor apprehensively stammered. "This ought to be interesting. It's the month I was born, exactly ten minutes before midnight of the *New Year*. In fact the exact time is right now," Walker observed as he reflexively glanced at the handsome gold-gilded clock positioned on the den's stone fireplace's Canadian oak mantel. 'Let's see what materializes!'

But then the worried mogul felt nauseous in his stomach. "I feel like vomiting," Walker admitted as he stared at the empty quart of *Johnny Walker Red* and at his empty crystal glass, both now situated on an adjacent den table. "I was a fool to drink so much scotch just because of this bogus bothersome television set," the multimillionaire confessed to himself.

Douglas Edwards seemed to be waiting for John P. Walker's undivided attention. Then the news broadcaster proceeded with the irrelevant December of '54 news items. "Senator Joseph McCarthy of Wisconsin was condemned by his colleagues in a special session for his misconduct during *Senate* committee meetings over the last several years. The flamboyant Republican

Senator had no remarks to make to the press concerning his recent formal reprimanding. In military news," Douglas Edwards proceeded, "*the U.S.S. Forrestal,* the largest warship ever built at almost sixty thousand tons, was christened and launched at the famous Newport News, Virginia shipyard."

At the sight of a champagne bottle being broken to officially launch the *Forrestal,* the mere thought of any type of alcoholic beverage made John P. Walker upchuck sour stomach juices from his upper digestive tract, which he sloppily wiped from his mouth. Nothing could now distract his eyes and the man's total concentration, all of which were intensely focused on the "evil 1954 *Emerson* television screen."

"On December 26th," Douglas Edwards matter-of-factly stated, "the *Cleveland Browns* convincingly defeated the *Detroit Lions* in the *NFL Championship* game, thus giving the Ohio city a much anticipated sports' championship that had eluded the baseball *Cleveland Indians* in the recent October *World Series. Browns* owner..."

Suddenly, the Emerson television screen went blank and then showed a series of alternating and fluttering horizontal and vertical lines. "What's goin' on?" John P. Walker moaned in his stupor. "This old set can't quit before it gets to my birthday! What about December 31st?" he mocked. "Come on you damned thing! Don't give up now!"

An image appeared on the television monitor but it wasn't the countenance of newscaster Douglas Edwards. Instead, a familiar voice from the past resonated from the *Emerson's* speaker. "Hello, this is John Cameron Swayze bringing you the *Camel News Caravan,* brought to you by *Camel* cigarettes. I'd walk a mile for a *Camel,*" Douglas Edwards' contemporary rival news commentator remarked.

John P. Walker foamed from his mouth as more sour stomach digestive liquid spewed up from his esophagus. The millionaire was in shock as he slouched down in his comfortable couch and half-heartedly listened to the new anchorman's enunciation.

"Our news program is coming to you tonight over Channel 13," John Cameron Swayze related to his almost incoherent audience of one. "Just before midnight tonight, December 31st, 1954, a deformed baby showing signs of mental retardation was born to Joseph and Louise Walker at the Atlantic City Hospital," the anchorman reported.

"That's impossible!" John P. Walker hiccupped. "As you can see, John Cameron Swayze, I'm perfectly fine! Hic! Don't try demeaning me! Hic!"

"Upon being taken home, the imperfect infant was immediately switched with the baby of Giles and Hillary Wood, loyal employees of Joseph and Louise Walker," Swayze reported. "As a result, Giles and Hillary Wood are the biological parents of John P. Walker and slow-learner' stable-boy Johnny Wood happens to be the sole legitimate son and heir of the now deceased Joseph and Louise Walker, the former owners of the lucrative Walker Asphalt and Tar Company of Hammonton, New Jersey."

"What!" John P. Walker balked at what he considered false news reporting. "My butler and my maid are my parents?" he gasped. "This terrible secret has been kept from me for almost forty-eight years!" he vociferously screamed. "And my poor mentally challenged lame stable-boy Johnny Wood is really supposed to be me, the original John P. Walker!"

John Cameron Swayze's all-too-sober form instantly dissolved upon the television screen. A moment of static and vertical and horizontal fluttering followed. Then the set mysteriously turned itself off.

At three minutes before midnight Giles and Hillary Wood entered the mansion's spacious den. Giles was carrying a bottle of vintage champagne to officially celebrate the arrival of the *New Year*. The pair immediately rushed to John Peter Walker's aid when they noticed his limp form slumped down upon the cranberry-colored soft leather sofa.

"My God Giles! What in the world has happened to him?" the maid yelled.

"There's no pulse! Hillary, there's no pulse I say!" Giles Wood shouted as he desperately felt his employer's wrists and throat. "He's dead! My God Hillary! I think he's dead!" Giles panted. "Either he had a massive heart attack or had choked on his own vomit! My God Hillary! He drank an entire quart of scotch!"

"Our son is dead! Giles! Our son is dead!" Hillary deliriously shrieked.

"Yes, and we have kept this ugly secret for too many years. Hillary, did you hear what I said?" Giles asked. "We've kept this secret for too many years! We had promised *his* parents never to tell it. And now this family tragedy has ended it all!"

"I'll call the rescue squad. Perhaps they can revive him," Hillary Wood' suggested to her all-too-formal husband. "Maybe *he* is in such a drunken state that it seems like his heart isn't beating!"

"No Hillary, not yet. Don't call the paramedics just yet!" Giles insisted. "I first have something I feel I must do. Our future deserves to be secure after all we've been through!"

Giles Wood swiftly paced out of the luxurious room, down the majestic wood-paneled corridor to the mansion's mammoth library. He swiveled a portrait of Mr. Joseph Walker to the right, exposing the combination knob to a huge wall safe. Putting on his clean white gloves, the knowledgeable butler repeated the combination he had memorized over the years, "Thirteen-left, thirteen-right, and now thirteen left."

"Giles, what on earth are you doing?" Hillary Wood demanded. "You're committing grand theft when *we* should be calling the rescue squad!"

"Hillary, all these pathetic years we've sacrificed and toiled for nothing," Giles ranted like a madman. "Our own son, our own flesh and blood has paid us shoddy minimum wages to be *his* exploited butler and *his* private domestic maid. At least his substitute parents showed us kindness and generosity in helping us send *their* physically impaired and mentally deficient son to special schools," the butler argued. "And all these years *we* have not been justly and fairly compensated for raising *their* lovable Johnny in the servant's cottage. And for the past thirteen years *we've* had to labor for the selfish whims of *our* own son, this egotistical dolt', who treated *us* as if we were illegal aliens or area indigents."

"Giles, this is evil what *you* are doing!" Hillary screamed, revealing a trace of her own guilty conscience. "Put the money back, I tell you. Giles, please put the money back in the safe!"

"The perfect crime!" Giles cackled as his hands held the stacks of hundred dollar bills that had been cached away in the concealed safe. "This is our retirement, Hillary. Our retirement ticket to tropical climates, do you hear?" Giles laughed deliriously. "This is finally our just compensation for what the Walker' family has done to our lives this past half-century!"

"What should I do?" Hillary begged her husband. "Should I call the authorities now?"

"Wait another ten minutes until I hide this cash in the servant's quarters," Giles advised his wife. "Then you can notify the rescue squad of Mr. Walker's untimely but warranted and propitious demise!"

"You mean of *our son's* demise," Hillary Wood sobbed.

"No Hillary, I meant Mr. Walker's demise!" Giles maintained. "No decent son would ever treat his parents like John Peter Walker has treated us these past miserable forty-eight years!"

"The Timeless Sports Car"

Henry Johnson was very content with his station in life. The man was a successful lawyer in his hometown of Hammonton, New Jersey and was looking forward to early retirement. Johnson had married his high school sweetheart Lois and the couple had three grown sons, Howard, Harry and Hugh. 'Howard is now ready to take over the family' law firm,' Henry Johnson thought as he stepped out onto the Bellevue Avenue/Horton Street pavement from *his* Attorney Office, 'and Harry is a prominent doctor at *Jefferson University Hospital* in Philly. And young Hugh is a prominent real estate developer in Saddle Brook up in North Jersey. What more could a 59 year-old man wish for?'

Once a month Henry Johnson would meet two cousins Charles "Chickie" Sceia and John Fallucca for lunch at a different pre-selected area restaurant. The three "paisons" would traditionally converge on a different eatery on the third Thursday and enjoy each other's company over burgers and frosted mugs of thirst-quenching draught beer.

'Last month's cousins' engagement was at the *Mill Street Pub* over in Mays Landing,' Henry thought, 'and today's lunch is at the *Great American Grille and Pub* in Hamilton Township,' the lawyer reminded himself as he sauntered to his tan *Lexus* parked around the corner on Horton Street. 'This time was *my* choice in the rotation so I know exactly where the restaurant is located. I can't wait to see Chickie and Johnny and discuss and solve the world's perplexing problems,' Johnson mused as he clicked the remote control unlocking his luxury automobile's driver-side door. 'I actually look forward to these once a month get-togethers.'

Henry Johnson steered his expensive car down Horton, made a right onto Orchard and then another right onto North Third Street. He stopped at the red traffic signal and proceeded straight ahead across Bellevue, and where Third' merged with Central Avenue at the yellow-brick *Hammonton Middle School*, the driver then took Central to *Route 30,* the *White Horse Pike*. In another five minutes the suave sociable lawyer was on Weymouth Road heading toward *Route 322,* the *Black Horse Pike*. 'I've ridden this highway at least three thousand times and know every inch of it,' Johnson mused.

Fifteen miles east on "the Pike" toward Atlantic City was a shopping center across from the newly constructed ultra-modern *Hamilton Mall*, and in that shopping center were shops and stores all having the same attractive brick façade, with one of the establishments being the aforementioned *Great American Grille and Pub*.

'Today we're scheduled to get together at 3:15,' Henry thought as he inserted a music disc into his dashboard panel and then listened to the *Billboard Top Rock 'n' Roll Hits of 1956*. '1956,' Henry imagined with a nostalgic smile. 'What a wonderful year! And what a horribly tragic year it was also!' the lawyer recalled.

The tan *Lexus* cruised past the huge *Atlantic Blueberry Company Farm, Mays Landing Division* on the right, and just before the sentimental '56 oldies *CD* finished playing its last selection, Henry maneuvered his well' equipped vehicle right off of *Route 322*. Then the hungry man made a sharp left turn and next drove behind an *I-Hop,* a *McDonald's* and a *KFC'* franchise. Soon Johnson was in the designated shopping center that featured a fine mixture of brick-façade stores, supermarkets and shops.

Henry checked his wristwatch and compared the time to the clock inside his fabulous car. '3:05,' he thought. 'I'll sit and wait here until Chickie or Johnny arrives. They're both usually pretty punctual, actually more punctual than pretty,' the good-humored fellow chuckled.

It was a warm April 24 day, and as Henry listened to his '50s music and adjusted his air-conditioning a few degrees cooler, he recollected the significance of the particular date. 'Lois and I were married on April 24th,' Johnson fondly remembered, 'and then there was that tragedy, that terrible tragedy that I don't want to think about ever again.'

The fastidious lawyer raised the volume to his 1956 oldies' *CD* and then after recollecting the horrible catastrophe that had occurred on April 24th of that same unforgettable year, Henry Johnson quickly switched the CD mode to a more contemporary John Fogerty album, *Premonition*.

Henry again checked his watch (impatiently awaiting the arrival of either Charles "Chickie" Sceia or Johnny Fallucca) in a nervous reflexive response to alleviate his temporary emotional anxiety. It was now 3:15, and neither cousin's vehicle had entered the parking lot facing the designated *Great American Grille and Pub.*

'It's very unlike either of them to miss our monthly appointment,' Henry reckoned as he attempted to make himself more comfortable in his light brown leather driver's seat. 'My cousins are both dependable fellas'. Something is definitely wrong here! But I'm not going to panic!'

Afternoon shoppers pulled into and others exited parking spaces to the left and right of Johnson', who now wondered what was keeping his cousins from promptly showing up. 'I'll wait here until 3:20 and then enter the restaurant,' Henry considered. 'They might already be seated inside enjoying cold draughts. But where are their cars? Maybe they came together in a new car I'm not familiar with?' Henry hypothesized. 'And in the past we've always had the courtesy of waiting outside in our autos' so that all three of us could enter together!'

Five more minutes elapsed and Henry was now feeling more than a bit apprehensive. He climbed out of his tan *Lexus*, paced across the asphalt and soon stepped onto the shopping center's sidewalk. The slightly concerned man opened the front door to the popular restaurant but only two patrons were seated at the bar and customers were occupying only three out of the four-dozen tables in the dining room. After glancing around the pub's interior several times, Henry felt awkward when he suddenly noticed the bartender and a curious waitress staring at him, so without initiating a conversation Johnson quickly abandoned the premises and shuffled back to the security of *his* tan *Lexus.*

'I'll wait here until 3:45,' Henry confided to his image in the rearview' mirror. 'It's so unlike either Chickie or Johnny to forget about our habitual monthly luncheon,' Johnson thought as he double-checked the date carefully written inside his monthly calendar book. 'I feel so stupid every time I call to remind them about the monthly late-lunch session. And Chickie and Johnny always tell me to remind my clients about court appointments and depositions and not to lecture *them* about honoring *our* monthly restaurant luncheons.'

3:45 arrived but cousins Chickie and Johnny had not. Henry Johnson reluctantly fired-up the tan *Lexus* sedan's engine, backed out of his parking space and soon was heading west on the *Black Horse Pike* back toward Hammonton. As Henry approached the landmark *Palace Diner* on the left, he was struck with a sudden inspiration. "I'll call cousin Johnny on *his* cell phone and give him a good friendly reprimand for failing to remember the *Great American Grille* lunch engagement. I got to get this weird anomaly out of my mind so that I can think straight. I hope that nothing unexpected happened to them!'

The somewhat distraught driver punched in the appropriate telephone number on his cell phone, touched the "Send" button and waited through three rings. Johnny Fallucca answered his portable cell phone on the fourth ring.

"Hello!" said the call's recipient.

"Johnny," Henry began in an imperative tone, "where the heck were you? I was parked outside the *Great American Grille* from 3:05 until 3:45, and neither you nor cousin Chickie showed up!" Johnson admonished. "I had always thought that you guys were supposed to be reliable mature adults!"

"Henry," Johnny replied with a degree of astonishment, "Chickie and I are sitting at the bar in the *Great American* Grille right now still waiting for *you* to show up. We're now feeling pretty happy nursing down *our* fourth frosted mugs. We were beginning to worry about you. From where are you calling? *Outer Space?"* Fallucca mildly chastised.

"That's impossible!" Henry ranted into his cell phone's specially installed overhead microphone attached to the driver's side sun-visor. "What time did *you* get there? And how long have you two clowns been sitting there?"

"Cousin Henny," Johnny amiably said, "we've both been sitting here at the bar since 3 p.m. waiting for you. Are you trying to pull some sinister trick on us? I think you're a little old to be playing silly high school pranks!" Johnny Fallucca joked. "Now what's the story from your end?"

"Believe me Johnny, I had entered the restaurant, looked all around, but only saw the lady bartender talking to two old gents that looked nothing like either you or Chickie," Henry maintained. "And there were only three tables occupied in the dining area, and neither you nor Chickie were in there. Did you guys ever get up and step to the *Men's Room* by any chance?"

"No! Never! Our kidneys are still in good condition," Johnny facetiously replied. "We were at the bar all the time and nowhere else. We figured we'd spot you right when you entered. You were right about one thing," Johnny told Henry. "There *were* two old geezers flirting with the woman bartender on the opposite side and she didn't like it one bit."

"Is this some sort of weird practical joke you two guys are playing?" Henry interrogated like the prosecutor he often was. "If so, it's not-too-funny and it's now very impractical and has worn out its impact!"

"Honest Henny, we're all mature grown men, related by common relative's blood and not inclined to play stupid juvenile pranks on one another," Johnny Fallucca declared as his voice shifted into a more serious tone. "Maybe it's time for *you* to visit your optometrist?"

"I'm sorry Johnny if I falsely accused you," Henry diplomatically apologized, "but where were your cars? They certainly weren't in the parking lot, or if they were," Johnson defensively continued, "I surely would've recognized them!"

"That's a mystery for sure," his cousin conceded. "They're parked in the lot as sure as Chickie and I are sitting and drinking at the bar right now!"

"Perhaps I really do need to have my eyes examined," Henry Johnson admitted to his honest and trustworthy cousin. "I'll schedule an appointment for early next week. I'm heading back toward Hammonton now and will see you fellas' Wednesday, May 22nd at 3:15 p.m. for a late lunch at *Sweetwater Casino* on the *Mullica River*. It's still my choice! And let's not mess this one up! Write it down right now!"

"Okay, I'll tell Chickie," Johnny lustily laughed. "Sweetwater Casino, Wednesday, May 22nd at 3:15 as usual. But why don't you just turn around and head back to the restaurant? It's no big deal, ya' know!"

"Thanks Johnny, but it's also my wedding anniversary and tonight I'm taking Lois and the three sons out to *Venice Plaza* over in Berlin to celebrate!" Johnson mentioned. "The place has a great gourmet chef so maybe it's a blessing in disguise for my delicate intestines that I'm missing a delicious lunch. I certainly don't want to over-exert my sensitive digestive system! Maybe a rain-check with you guys is in good order."

"All right Henny," Johnny chuckled, "go out with the family and have a terrific time. I'll tell Chickie here your' very strange but entertaining story. And please tell Lois and the boys we said 'hi', and don't forget about May 22nd, 3:15 p.m. at Sweetwater. Don't mess up this time! See ya' cousin!"

"Bye Johnny and tell that occasional alcoholic Chickie I said 'hi'," Johnson jested and answered while shaking his head in disbelief at the very weird non-meeting that had recently been discussed over the phone.

Just as Henry Johnson pressed *End* on his car phone, he realized that he had gone straight in the fork in the road, and instead of veering off left taking County Road 553 toward Hammonton', he was now en route to the village of Elwood.

"Oh well, I guess a minor detour is just what I need to top-off a rather peculiar afternoon," Henry said to his aging silver-haired reflection in the rear-view mirror. "Maybe the hamlet of Elwood has blossomed into a major metropolis since the last time I've been there," the driver snickered. "I haven't traveled this back country hick road in many years even though it's only eleven or so miles from Hammonton."

The rather disgusted fellow tapped the dashboard *CD* indicator to change his music preference from John Fogerty's *Premonition* album back to the *Billboard Top Rock 'n' Roll Hits of 1956*. Dark storm clouds were observable to the west toward Philadelphia along with occasional lightning flashes and peals of thunder rumbling in the distance. Johnson raised the volume to his '50s music to escape his present perplexity and then he mentally navigated back to the year 1956.

'I seldom take this remote road,' Henry thought. 'In fact I can't recall the last time I had', possibly it *was* as far back as 1956. Oh well, and I guess I just have to accept the inevitability of April showers.'

The tan *Lexus* rounded a bend on the right and the first object that came into Henry Johnson's view was a magnificent white 1956 *Thunderbird* convertible with a splendid *Continental* wheel cover on its back. The impressive shiny classic sports car was situated on the front lawn of an old white bungalow that was in desperate need of several coats of paint, appearing to have been built during the *WWII* era.

"What a beauty!" Henry gasped as he slammed on the brakes. "It's got red interior just like the one I had wanted back in '56, but Dad quickly put an end to my fantasy by making me drive his black '53 *Pontiac* around Hammonton."

Henry carefully backed up his tan *Lexus* in order to gain a better inspection of the marvelous white vintage automobile that appeared to be in mint condition. A poster attached under the left windshield wiper blade read "Like New: Only $20,000.00!"

The clever lawyer clambered out of his luxury vehicle to admire the white relic from *his* past. 'I've got to have this baby!' the examiner covetously thought as he stuck his fingers inside the convertible's interior and touched the well-preserved red leather upholstery. 'I couldn't own it back in '56 but I sure have the means to acquire this great roadster now!'

An old farmer in a checkered red and black flannel shirt and grimy blue jeans came ambling out to greet the prospective customer. "Howdy Mister!" the elderly whiskered gentleman said. "I'm Brent Wagner, the owner of this here perfectly reconditioned *T-bird*. Isn't it' a beauty!"

"Sure is!" Henry marveled and concurred. "I really wanted one of these bad when I was a rambunctious teenager. Trouble was that my dad was a very frugal practical man, even though he could've easily afforded to purchase one for me. I'm not quite as economical as my Pop was."

"Well son, if you're that interested, ya' can have it for a mere twenty thousand," the old farmer stated. "And that's a real bargain, yes sir-eeee it is! This honey's only got seventy-three thousand original miles on it. Belonged to my brother-in-law who left it to me in *his* will," Brent Wagner emphasized. "Now I have no use for this classy toy so I figured I'd convert it into quick cash to spruce-up my bungalow a bit."

Henry walked back to his tan *Lexus*, reached inside and shut off its engine. His desire was to negotiate a lower selling price to claim his heart's desire. 'I'm going to buy this *T-bird* if it's the last thing I do!' the man mentally promised his greedy eyes. 'Maybe I can haggle the old gent down a bit!'

The elderly man pulled a toothpick from his toothless mouth and uttered, "Say stranger, I'm gonna' start the engine up and you'll notice that this here baby purrs like a kitten. Still got a lot of zip, too, I must admit!"

"I'll give you eighteen thousand dollars for it right now!" Henry offered. "I'll gladly write you out a check for that amount right this minute! I always pay everything by check for obvious income tax purposes. That's why Mr. Wagner I always have my checkbook readily available."

"Wait a minute!" the shrewd old codger replied. "I wanted cash on the barrelhead, not a damned check! The *IRS* will take me to the cleaners with a check, yes they will!" Brent Wagner argued. "If ya' want to pay by check, the price is twenty-five thousand to allow for federal taxes."

"If it will start and can be driven, I'll give you twenty-five thousand," Henry reluctantly responded with a trace of regret in his voice for compromising *his* already set purchasing price. But in his heart, Johnson aptly knew that money was no object in realizing his fondest and grandest teenage dream come true.

The old gentleman entered the car, reached into his pocket and removed a set of keys on a ring', one of which he inserted into the ignition. With one twist of his right wrist, the white *Thunderbird* started up and sounded as good as new.

"I'll take it!" Henry enthusiastically agreed as he watched lightning flashing and heard thunder rolling to the west in the direction of Philadelphia. "You certainly drive a hard bargain! I must say!"

"How do I know that this here check you're gonna' cut me isn't gonna' bounce?" the old man challenged. "I've been burned several times before with lesser amounts!"

"Because I'm a lawyer in Hammonton and I have a family name and a good personal reputation to maintain!" the attorney argued. "I can't afford to write a bogus check because then my last name would be Mud instead of Johnson."

"Johnson? Hammonton lawyer! I've heard of you," the old farmer acknowledged with a forced grin. "Ya' do have a good name around these parts, I'll admit to that. Show me your driver's license with your name and address on it and then I'll sell this here precious jewel to ya'!"

Henry Johnson showed old Brent Wagner *his* bona fide New Jersey driver's license, which matched the identity the lawyer had originally claimed to be. The elated old backwoods resident stuck his head inside the sports car and opened the passenger side hatch and inserted a second key into the T-bird's glove compartment and then he removed the automobile's "Bill of Sale." "I was comin' out here to shut the windows just when ya' stopped because it looks like rain coming this way!" Wagner informed Henry.

Henry Johnson was quite familiar with the transition of a standard car ownership document, and after the men signed the required signatures in the appropriate places, the deal had been officially consummated. Henry then wrote out a check for the prescribed amount to the now ecstatic Brent Wagner, and the two men shook hands to recognize the transaction.

"Ya' gonna' come back and pick it up?" the seller asked his euphoric newfound customer.

"Why yes," Henry confidently indicated. "I'll return later this afternoon with one of my sons and we'll pick it up and take it back to Hammonton. It'll be a glorious anniversary surprise for my wife Lois."

Henry eagerly walked the fifteen feet to his tan *Lexus,* opened the driver's side door and entered his distinctive automobile. Upon turning the ignition key, for some remote reason, the electrical system did not respond. Henry tried five times to start the engine but to no avail.

The lawyer exited his auto' and noticed that Brent Wagner was still watching him. "These new cars and their sophisticated computer systems," Henry moaned to the backwoods shack owner. "Sometimes I think that modern technology is actually going backwards."

"I know exactly what ya' mean!" Brent Wagner verified. "Give me a four-barrel carburetor with a *V-8* engine any day over this here fancy fuel-injection *V-6* stuff! I ain't never had no problem with this here *T-bird* nor with my '53 *Chevy* parked behind the house. Say Mister," Brent continued, "how would ya' like to leave your *Lexus* parked on my lawn and drive the *T-Bird* home. Then you and a mechanic can return here and tow your fancy machine back to Hammonton."

"Terrific idea," agreed Henry. "I'll be able to skirt the thunderstorms because I'll be heading northwest toward Elwood while the thunder and lightning seems to be going southeast toward Williamstown."

Brent Wagner neatly folded the twenty-five thousand-dollar check' in half and placed it in the upper-left-pocket of his red and black checkered flannel shirt. The two men then pushed the tan *Lexus* onto the weed-infested unkempt front lawn as Henry guided its forward progress by vigorously turning the steering wheel to the right.

After the *Lexus* had been moved a safe distance off the country road and onto the unkempt lawn, the two men again shook hands. Johnson forgot all about his disabled *Lexus,* opened the *T-bird's* door and happily leaped inside. The now-mobile-again lawyer waved "goodbye" to the grateful old fellow as *he* pulled away heading northwest toward the hamlet of Elwood.

'This *T-bird* is timeless!' Henry thought as he watched the seemingly accurate speedometer needle rise up to fifty. 'It's just as beautiful and graceful in 2002 as it had been back in '56. I'll be the envy of everyone in town!'

Henry casually turned the sports car's radio knob to determine if the device still worked. He was both rewarded and shocked when his ears perceived the familiar voice of a Philadelphia *DJ* from the past, *his* past. Joe Niagra's baritone said, "Thanks for listening to *WIBG*, Philly's top rock and roll radio station, and the only boss sound in town. This rockin' bird is about to fly. Now here's a blast from the past, a knocked-out Niagra nifty! Here comes Bill Haley and the Comets singing and playing the teen *National Anthem,* 'Rock Around the Clock'."

'This has got to be a commercial or a cruisin' record promo' of some sorts!' Henry Johnson imagined. His eyes briefly glanced at the radio and observed that the dial was set on *AM 99*, the exact position of *WIBG,* Philadelphia back in the nifty '50s. 'This just *has* to be a flashback commercial,' *his* naturally skeptical mind again thought.

In total amazement, the baffled driver turned the radio knob and found a news broadcast in progress. "And in entertainment news," the announcer declared, "*My Fair Lady*, a smash hit musical by Alan Jay Lerner and Frederick Lowe is proving to be a fantastic box-office attraction at the *Mark Hellinger Theater* in New York. The popular *Broadway* play is based on George Bernard Shaw's classic story *Pygmalion,* and the terrific new musical features talented stage stars Rex Harrison and Julie Andrews. In other national entertainment news, ..."

Henry Johnson turned the radio dial and momentarily heard Carl Perkins singing *his* famous rendition of "Blue Suede Shoes," and then the disbelieving driver quickly rotated the knob to another news broadcast. "The *Marine Corps* has finally finished investigating the drowning of six recruits at Parris Island, South Carolina while a platoon was on a so-called 'disciplinary march'. Sergeant Matthew C. McKeon has been convicted of drinking on duty and found guilty of negligent homicide. His rank has been reduced to *Private*. In other news," the radio announcer continued, "the *New York Coliseum* is scheduled to open on April 28th. The new *Coliseum* will indeed be the world's largest

26

exhibition building, covering over nine acres at a phenomenal cost of over 35 million dollars. In other current news, Victor Riesel was blinded when…"

Henry neurotically turned the radio dial back to *WIBG Radio 99* and heard Joe Niagra gleefully shout, "And now here's Elvis Presley's smash-hit recording of the classic rhythm and blues number Heartbreak Hotel!" Henry listened to the song's familiar intro', and then turned the *T-bird's* dial to "OFF."

'This is impossible!' the highly alarmed driver evaluated. 'I must be caught in some kind of time vacuum, a puzzling time warp! There's definitely one way I can prove that my theory is correct and I'm going to test my idea.'

Henry drove his new white *Ford Thunderbird* convertible (with the top down) into downtown Hammonton, which to his astonishment was downtown Hammonton, vintage 1956. 'Oh my God!' Henry thought. 'There's *Godfrey's Drugstore* on the corner. That business disappeared in the early sixties, and over there is *J.J. Newberry's* five and ten, and *Miller's Department Store*, and all of the soda fountains I used to enjoy so much as a kid. And look, the *Rivoli Theater's* marquee is visible down the street, and *Fire Company #1* is still in the middle of town and not out on Lincoln and Passmore Avenues! And all of the cars on Bellevue Avenue are 1956 and earlier.'

The driver steered his *Thunderbird* to the right and onto Central Avenue. He parked his 'wheels' on the street outside of *Olivo's Supermarket* and ambled across Central to his favorite teenage hangout, the *Gem Burger Palace*. Seated inside booths and at the counter were carefree *Hammonton High School* students' eating burgers, chatting the latest gossip and listening to jukebox tunes. The boys were wearing their white and blue trimmed lettermen's sweaters and most of the girls were costumed in blue and white cheerleader uniforms with black and white saddle shoes while other looser and tougher-looking young females were wearing pink and black *Poodle* skirts.

As Henry's eyes scanned the very active teen' scene he noticed his future wife Lois gossiping with *his* best friend, Tommy Davidson and *her* best friend, head cheerleader Candy Taylor. And also congregated inside the hangout were Bob Simpson, Chet Douglas, Dave Jensen and Jim Parker, all teammates of Henry's on the fearsome *Hammonton High School* football team, but none of them recognized their good friend's bearded face and silver-haired middle-age appearance.

Henry's mind was in a state of complete bewilderment as he approached the main counter where several of his old chums were sitting on stools discussing various topics. Mr. Clyde Dawkins, the gem's proprietor asked Johnson where he had gotten the "strange light blue jeans" *he* was wearing.

"Oh," Henry said with a smile and a blush on his cheeks, "my Mom put them in the washing machine and they faded when she used too much bleach. Maybe I'm starting a new fad?" he joked. "What do ya' think?"

"You're still living with your' mother?" Mr. Dawkins inquired and criticized shaking his head in mock disgust. "Why Mister, I think *you* look like you're about sixty years old!"

Henry heard his former high school friends Bob Simpson and Chet Douglas laughing on their main counter stools in response to Mr. Dawkins typical sarcasm. Feeling embarrassed and a bit disoriented, Henry Johnson rushed out of the establishment and hopped into his newly acquired *Thunderbird* as he heard Jim Lowe's "The Green Door" blasting from the *Gem's* jukebox speakers.

"I need more verification of my new reality!" the mentally disheveled driver said to himself. "Either I'm cracking up in a major mental meltdown or I *have* already cracked up!" The time-traveler turned on the ignition and motored around the block to another familiar old Hammonton haunt where he had bought dozens of automobile magazines and comic books in his youth.

Henry parked his *T-bird* outside of *Dan's Stationery Store,* which in 2002 had the designation *Tapper's Stationery.* He briskly stepped inside the establishment and checked the date on the newspapers, and it was indeed April 24th, 1956. Johnson glanced at the saleswoman behind the counter and at a customer purchasing a pack of *Lucky Strike* cigarettes. "That will be thirty cents Mr. Flemming," the woman politely informed.

'Why that's Mr. Flemming the local electrician buying the cigarettes and the lady behind the counter is Mrs. Martha Merlino, Lois's aunt! Those people died in the 1970s! I even attended Mr. Flemming's and Aunt Martha's funerals!' Henry remembered. 'I really *am* back in 1956!'

Johnson exited *Dan's Stationery Store* in a hurry. The date April 24th, 1956 was now a nagging nightmare that had been lingering in the back of the man's mind. Henry's father, Dennis Johnson had been killed at precisely 5:30 on that date on Moss Mill Road while changing a tire. He had been struck by a speeding tractor-trailer that had veered off the roadway. 'If everything else is correct in this time warp, I have more than enough time to make it to Moss Mill Road and save Dad!' the time traveler reckoned while intensely scrutinizing his wristwatch.

The driver of the '56 *Thunderbird* sped around the corner to Egg Harbor Road, briefly stopped and then turned left. Henry's new old car zoomed past *Hammonton Lake Park* where a *Little League* game was in progress and then turned left again onto Moss Mill Road. Soon Johnson had crossed the *White Horse Pike* (which now had a 'Stop Sign' and no traffic light) and was heading east toward Egg Harbor City.

When the auto's speedometer registered fifty-six miles an hour, the dashboard lights automatically and mysteriously flicked on and the time clock coincidentally indicated that it was nearly five p.m. 'I still have a half-hour to rescue Dad!' Henry hypothesized. 'If I act quickly, I can save *his* life! I *will* save his life!'

Henry mashed his foot down on the accelerator and the *T-bird* responded with an instant burst of power. The driver recalled the year 1956, and a newsreel of events paraded through his unsettled mind as he sped east. Besides his father's accidental death, Henry had graduated *Hammonton High School* and had been accepted at the *University of Pennsylvania's School of Law*. He had been aggressively dating Lois Morgano and the two had expected to be married in April of 1960.

'I still have plenty of time to prevent the accident,' the owner of the marvelous time-vehicle evaluated. 'I want to get the tire changed before that tractor-trailer arrives or before that thunderstorm on the western horizon hits Moss Mill Road.'

As Henry Johnson drove further down the two-lane county highway he recalled that Dennis Johnson had only been thirty-eight years of age when *he* had met *his* tragic death. 'Dad would be eighty-four if he were still alive,' the determined son concluded. 'I'll make sure that *he* lives to see that age!'

Up ahead on the right a black '53 *Pontiac* sedan was situated on Moss Mill Road's right-hand shoulder. A middle-aged gentleman in a dark blue business suit was preoccupied jacking up the left rear-wheel. Henry halted his immaculate white *Thunderbird*, shut off the motor and got out to render his benign assistance. Saving his father's life was paramount in the time-traveler's mind.

"Hello," Henry greeted his beleaguered father. "I'll help you get that tire changed in a jiffy. You're in a business suit and I'm sure you don't want to get any grease or grime on it!"

"Why thank you sir," Dennis Johnson answered, not recognizing his oldest son sporting a beard, mustache and a distinguished middle-aged appearance. "My oldest son wants a white *T-bird* just like yours," Mr. Johnson related. "I don't think he's quite ready to have such a fancy car yet, if ya' know what I mean. I don't want to spoil any of my sons by giving them what they can't afford to buy on their own!"

"I understand completely," Henry stated. "I had to work long and hard to get the money to purchase *my* new car. Tell your son it's well-worth having and saving for."

Henry picked up the lug-wrench off of the ground and loosened the nuts holding the tire to the wheel. Then he methodically jacked the black *Pontiac* up to the desired height', removed the rim's lug nuts and pulled the deflated tire off the wheel.

"Ya' sure know what you're doing," Dennis Johnson sincerely complimented. "I hope that all three of my sons grow up to be just as helpful and as courteous as you are!"

"One thing's for sure," Henry joked. "A flat tire's only flat on the bottom. But I'm sure your sons will grow-up to be fine outstanding citizens," Henry assured his appreciative listener. "Apples and acorns don't fall far from the family tree! Are you on your way to a business meeting?"

"Yes, as a matter of fact I am," Mr. Dennis Johnson answered. "I'm goin' to Egg Harbor City for the *Atlantic County Bar Association's* annual dinner meeting. My wife has a *Civic Association* meeting over in Hammonton, so I'm goin' alone. Good thing she's missed all this aggravation! All because of one misplaced nail I suppose!"

Soon Henry had the spare tire (that his father had already taken out of the trunk) onto the rear wheel. He placed and then tightened the new rim's lug nuts onto the corresponding protruding bolt threads and after lowering the black *Pontiac* to the road's shoulder', he finished tightening up the lug-nuts using the tire iron.

Lightning began flashing to the west over downtown Hammonton, so Dennis Johnson figured he'd lift the damaged tire and deposit it inside the automobile's trunk.

Suddenly a tractor-trailer came rumbling around the bend and Dennis Johnson yelled for the helpful middle-age citizen to "Get out of the way!" The driver of the gigantic truck blasted *his* air-horn and heavily applied the brakes. The enormous rig's tires screeched on the highway's asphalt as its air brakes locked.

Henry Johnson stood petrified for a moment and then attempted jumping out of the path of the oncoming monstrosity. The tractor-trailer's right front fender clipped the victim and then the *Good Samaritan's* body hurtled over the black *Pontiac* and landed twelve feet away inside the fringe of a pine forest.

A Hammonton ambulance arrived twenty minutes later and transported the unfortunate highway helper to *Atlantic City Hospital.* The victim was pronounced dead and the attending doctors on duty reported to newspaper journalists that the man had sustained multiple injuries that had caused massive internal bleeding.

* * * * * * * * * * * *

On April 24th, 2002 Dennis Johnson, an eighty-four-year-old retired attorney made a wrong turn after leaving the *Black Horse Pike* not far from a traffic light adjacent to *Palace Diner.*

"Dennis," his wife said, "you should have turned left at the fork and gone back to Hammonton. Now you're going to wind-up in Elwood."

"Big deal Lois!" the stubborn elderly man gruffly replied. "So what if I missed the hypotenuse of the old right triangle! We'll just detour five miles out of our way, Lois. I seldom travel this back road. That's all we'll have to do to get to Elwood and then we'll take *Route 30* west to Hammonton. Anyway my dear wife, I really enjoy driving my new tan *Lexus*. Ya' know Lois," Dennis Johnson proceeded, "we don't have many more years left on this Earth to relish the wonderful material comforts life has to offer."

"You're so philosophical," the wife observed and commended. "You've always been that way, even in high school. I think that's one reason I married you!"

A mile ahead old Dennis Johnson observed a white '56 *Thunderbird* convertible with red interior parked on an unkempt lawn in front of an old wooden-frame country bungalow. The elderly driver immediately applied the brakes.

"Why are you stopping?" Lois Johnson asked her rejuvenated husband.

"Lois, our oldest son always wanted a white '56 *Thunderbird* but I was too stubborn to buy one for him. And once a stranger stopped on this very day in 1956 and helped me change a tire over on Moss Mill Road. The poor man was killed when he was hit by an out-of-control tractor-trailer just before a terrible thunderstorm hit. I'll never forget that violent accident Lois and I'll never forget that horrible afternoon!"

"You never told me about a man being killed!" the wife returned.

"I was so upset that I never found out his name from the police and never even called *his* family or attended *his* funeral," the elderly man informed his wife. "And I've felt guilty ever since that day."

"Then you're going to buy that beautiful white car?" the wife asked in a very surprised tone of voice.

"I sure am Lois," Dennis Johnson verified. "I sure am!"

"A Literary Dispute"

Thomas Eugene Barclay stepped from the Philadelphia Avenue pavement and entered a familiar Egg Harbor City, New Jersey dental office for his bi-annual check-up and teeth cleaning. The retired high school English teacher was enjoying his first September removed from the daily emotional pressure and mental tedium of instructing a hundred and thirty hormone-driven students at *Oakcrest High School*. Now *Labor Day* meant just another holiday on the hanging kitchen calendar.

"Good morning Mr. Barclay," the courteous and efficient receptionist/secretary greeted the new arrival at the dentist's office. "It's been a full half year since I've last seen you. Hope you haven't gotten any cavities in the last six months!"

"Hello Mrs. Carver," Tom cheerfully answered. "I believe I have a ten-thirty appointment for a cleaning. Since I'm not stressed-out from teaching I no longer feel like I have a giant cavity in the center of my head and now I can schedule an appointment any time of the day I feel it would be convenient for me," the at ease fellow said. "It's a really great feeling Jill! Freedom is a tremendous new sensation that I'm readily adapting to and also relishing. I can't wait until my wife retires from teaching so that then we could do plenty of traveling and vacationing."

"Right you are," the pert middle-age blonde-haired secretary replied. "Dr. Marshal should be finished with his present patient in about five minutes. How does it feel to be living without the pressure of daily work responsibilities? I'll bet it's a wonderful departure from the duress of rascally high school kids."

"Really terrific," the former educator said as he reached over and grabbed a slightly wrinkled business magazine from a floor rack. "I can now pursue my writing career without any school jobs interfering with my goals. I always seriously wanted to be an author and now's my big chance to see what I can accomplish. In fact I'm now in the process of polishing up a few old manuscripts I had written several decades ago."

"What are you writing?" Jill Carver curiously inquired as she looked up from her computer screen. "You don't seem to be the type involved with romance novels! My guess is either action/adventure or science fiction."

"Oh, I thought you knew," Barclay coyly stated. "I already have ten e-books on the *Internet* listed at *Amazon.com, Barnes and Noble* and at *Mobipocket.* I'm doing pretty well overall, if I might add," Tom modestly boasted. "Besides *Mobipocket*, which incidentally is universally used for all hand-held computer devices, my books also come in *Microsoft Reader* and *Adobe Reader* downloading e-book formats and soon they'll be available in paperback and hardcover editions too."

"Sounds pretty impressive," Mrs. Carver politely said. "But do you write romance or mystery novels? That's what I really enjoy reading. I honestly really can't get into westerns, fantasy books and murder stories."

"Right now Jill I have three young adult fantasy novels, two collections of novellas, three satires and two fairly decent adult-oriented novels on the market," Tom Barclay proudly revealed to the receptionist/secretary. "I had to wait until the state pension board cleared my name to receive monthly checks. Now I'm just a regular ordinary citizen walking around Egg Harbor just like a regular adult and thank goodness I'm no longer an obedient public servant," Thomas Barclay indicated and emphasized, "and I can now publish my adult novels and paranormal stories without fear of moral charges being advanced against me by the local school board bureaucrats or kids' crazy parents."

Jill Carver smiled and blushed in response to Tom Barclay's blunt evaluation of *his* particular writing genres and authoring style. Barclay' now considered himself a "free man" and no longer a slave to arbitrary school board mandates and to petty school administrative edicts. The former literature and grammar instructor believed that *his* novels and stories were directed toward three distinct reading audiences: young adult fiction, science fiction/paranormal enthusiasts and to men and women that preferred "adult-oriented" literature featuring adult language and content. The former pedagogue emphasized to Mrs. Carver that he had now evolved above and beyond picayune public criticism and ridiculous community censorship.

A pretty brunette dental assistant exited her work area, entered the receptionist's sitting room and cheerfully announced, "Mr. Barclay, Dr. Marshal is now ready to clean your teeth and to check your gums and molars," the attractive woman said while holding Tom's dental records in an oak tag folder. "If you will, please follow me into the second room."

Tom carefully inserted the wrinkled business magazine back into its floor rack and casually sauntered into the interior office walking behind the very pleasant auburn-haired dental technician. After getting into the dreaded leather reclining examination chair, the efficient employee adjusted Tom to the desired horizontal height and then skillfully placed and expertly hooked a bib around the literary patient's neck.

"Tom Barclay Shakespeare, how are you doing?" a familiar voice belonging to a middle-aged man that had just entered the room joked and wanted to know.

"Oh, Doc' Marshal. I'd recognize that baritone anywhere," the patient returned. "I'm doing just fine. And how about yourself? Keeping busy?"

"I'm just feeling great!" Dr. James Marshal replied. "Tom, aside from your checkup visit there's something I just gotta' tell you. I finally have those twelve stories finished I was telling you about. I'd like you to read them over if you have the time. When you leave, I'll give them to you. Remember the deal we had made over the telephone six months ago," the dentist reminded his captivated audience of one lying in the dental chair. "You'll thoroughly edit and proofread them, and then I'll give you fifteen percent of royalties if and when I can find a publisher."

"Okay Doc'," the amiable literature authority sincerely answered. "I'll look them over and give you an honest opinion sometime within the next few days. But I'm working on a few writing projects of my own. I'll tell you what. I'll see what I can do and give you some honest opinions, let's say in three weeks. I'm sure you can write a lot better than most of the students I had to teach over the course of the last three and a half decades."

After the perfunctory dental cleaning and gum examination had been accomplished, Dr. Jim Marshal handed Tom Barclay a rectangular cardboard box containing his precious twelve novellas that *he* had arduously labored two years developing. "Let me know what you think of my fiction work," Dr. Marshal requested. "I'm just a novice and can handle constructive criticism."

"Don't worry," the genial patient replied with a bright new smile. "You'll have my professional assessment in less than a month now that I have the time to relax and exclusively read for leisure and for pleasure."

After merrily saying 'goodbye' to affable Jill Carver', whose desk was encumbered with a pyramid of paperwork, bills and insurance forms stacked a full foot high, the jolly former English teacher exited the dentist's office and ambled around the corner to his modest light green *Mazda Protégé*. 'When those fat *Internet* royalty checks begin rolling in,' Barclay mused, 'then I'll finally be' able to afford a decent automobile. I'll read Doc' Marshal's stories but truthfully, I hardly have time since I'm so involved in completing my own work.'

The newly appointed "editor" drove his *Mazda* off of Philadelphia Avenue and turned east heading toward Buffalo Avenue and his middle-class stucco ranch home. 'Most of Egg Harbor's major streets are named after American cities,' the driver reviewed in his mind. 'There's Philadelphia, Buffalo, New York, Norfolk, Chicago, St. Louis, Boston, San Francisco and Cincinnati' Avenues, just to name a few. Real creative and original names, I must confess, and they all monotonously run parallel to one another,' the man mildly criticized as he motored to his modest residence. 'I only hope that Doc Marshal's stories demonstrate more fundamental originality than the mediocre names of these Egg Harbor avenues and streets do. On the other hand,' the carefree man thought and more rationally considered, 'there does exist some deviation in the street names with the European influence of London, Liverpool, Heidelberg, Antwerp and Bremen Avenues.'

And after preparing and then eating a ham and cheese on rye sandwich for lunch, Tom decided to examine the first of Dr. Marshal's novellas, which was appropriately titled "The Marionette." Halfway through the interesting tale, Barclay thought, 'Doc' really has an excellent imagination. It's too bad he doesn't have a much-needed writing voice along with a distinctive writing style and his story is almost devoid of dialogue,' the writing authority concluded and mentally critiqued. 'It's also unfortunate that this novella lacks vital focus and good narrative description but I believe I can convert it into quality literature. In fact,' Tom thought, "I know I can enhance and embellish this story. Everyone thinks that just because *they* can write two hundred plausible pages to make a book-length manuscript that they have written *good* fiction. I can doctor this baby-up for Dr. Marshal and convert it into a more than adequate professional manuscript.'

Tom Barclay alertly spent the entire afternoon editing the first twenty-page novella, conscientiously deleting dull hackneyed language, modifying poor word choices, eliminating obvious idiomatic expressions and cliches and then inserting more appropriate nomenclature as well as correcting and changing glaring spelling, grammar and punctuation mistakes. 'It's a good thing this "Marionette" story is double-spaced because there're so many errors I have to repair or adjust. But the story ideas are basically satisfactory,' Tom believed, 'and I can make the main characters sound less artificial and have them behave like real non-plastic people rather than appear being shallow, hollow and one-dimensional to the reader.'

"The editor" labored industriously all afternoon and then Tom marched down the hall to *his* revered "office," which was once his oldest son's bedroom, and Barclay immediately sat down in his sanctuary's captain's swivel chair situated behind his sacred computer screen and began performing a minor miracle on Doctor Marshal's creative endeavor.

Word by word, sentence by sentence, paragraph by paragraph and page by page Tom assiduously retyped the entire story manuscript (that had been typewritten without margins) into Microsoft Word, adding pertinent detail, description, transitions, coherency, settings, in-depth character portrayal and analysis and necessary plot enhancement to "The Marionette."

'Most people think that they can sit down and write a story once and make it good, but being a former teacher,' Tom pondered, 'I realize from ample experience that a story must be rewritten and edited at least four times to be brought up to snuff. That's a vitally necessary painstaking procedure to undertake to distinguish its identity and its unique characteristics from the remainder of the stories out there. Not everyone is a literary Mozart that can get a composition right in one sitting.'

Laura Barclay came home from work at 3:45, entered the end bedroom "office" and gave her husband a small peck on the cheek. "Hi Honey!" she greeted. "Working on your first best-selling novel?"

"Oh hi Laura. How was school today?" Tom asked changing the subject. "Any discipline problems or hostile parent conferences? I don't miss those unpleasant scenarios one bit."

"It's a lot easier teaching fourth grade at *St. Nicholas* even though I don't get nearly the salary I was getting when I was working at the local public school," Laura Barclay acknowledged. "But Tom, I don't have to tell you that the aggravation and the stress aren't nearly as great and the kids in general at the parochial school are so much better behaved."

"I'm happy you quit the public school even though it's harder for us to make ends meet," the husband supportively agreed. "I spent thirty-five years in the educational trenches trying to civilize four thousand-plus rambunctious high school students, so I've paid my dues and then some. When I die and trek over to the pearly gates," the husband proceeded and predicted, "St. Peter's going to say to me, 'Tom Barclay. You've dedicated thirty-five years of your life to try and educate four thousand teenagers. Forget walking up the colossal spiral marble staircase. Hop into the elevator and take the express route up to heaven'!"

"Sometimes you're so funny and clever," Laura casually complimented. "What are you working on Tom? Another dynamic *Internet* e-book?"

"No Honey," her spouse reluctantly answered. "I'm doing a favor for Dr. Jim Marshal. I promised our family dentist I would edit *his* manuscript, but instead I like this story 'The Marionette' so much that I'm actually not only rewriting it, I'm ghostwriting it. This thing has great potential Laura," the aspiring author asserted, "and if I can get it out into the public domain, then I think it could make a sensational television special or even a medium-range-budget *Hollywood* movie."

"I always said you missed your calling," Laura responded sporting a supportive grin. "You should've been a successful writer Tom even though you had devoted three and a half decades of your life to teaching and evaluating your students' inferior compositions. Now finally your avocation can be your vocation. Are Dr. Marshal's stories copyrighted?" Laura asked. "He seems like the type that would go to that extreme."

"Yes they are, but it really doesn't make any big difference," Tom knowingly replied. "This copyrighting business is all overrated. The stories that Jim gave me, although quite unique, are not of generally accepted publishing standards' quality. But Laura, I honestly like this first tale so much that I'm going to convert it into superior world-class literature, and I suspect I'll enjoy working on the eleven other selections just as much as I

38

will rewriting this first one that seems to have a little Edgar Allan Poe in it blended in with a trace of Jack London."

"Okay Honey, as long as you know what you're doing," the amenable wife agreed. "Just make sure you get proper credit for your active involvement in Dr. Marshal's dream project. I'm sure *he'll* immediately recognize your valuable input when he sees the finished product. For one thing on the positive side Tom, he's a professional person to start with and not your common everyday con-artist. You got to regard that as a plus."

The following afternoon Tom Barclay delivered the highly improved version of "The Marionette" to Dr. James P. Marshal's dentist office. "Thanks Tom," the teeth, gum and mandible specialist said. "I'll read it over tonight and tell you what I think of your edit. I'll also tell you whether I think it's worth fifteen percent of the pie," the doctor chuckled. "Writing is just a hobby to me but if one of my stories clicks with an agent or editor, then I might soon have to grapple with a new profession on my hands," the amateur author disclosed.

"I added some detail, character traits and I also concentrated a lot of my energy on your plot development," Tom solemnly answered. "Now Jim, you'll have to understand that for a story to ever become superior literature, it must be meticulously scrutinized, read, revised and rewritten at least three more times," Tom specified and emphasized. "In the writing business, only three percent of the best authors make the big bucks at the summit of the mammoth writing pyramid, and to get there and stay there at the top of the matrix Jim, ya' gotta' be better than the other ninety-seven percent vigorously tryin' to dethrone you. The writing business is more competitive than you can imagine."

"I'll have to remember that advice and file it away for future reference," the dentist assured the teacher-turned-author. "I'll give you a buzz later tonight with my reaction to your edit. I can't wait to re-read this baby!"

That same late summer evening the phone rang at the Barclay residence. Tom saw the name Dr. James Marshal appear on his caller *ID* and anxiously picked-up the receiver from its cradle. "Hello Jim," Tom said. "How's it going?"

"Great Tom," the dentist confirmed. "Say, you've really done a fantastic job editing 'The Marionette.' It's like you installed the exact same words in just the right places that I wish I could have thought of while organizing it. You're a literary genius Tom and I mean that compliment sincerely. I gotta' admit that you're one heck of an editor."

"Well Jim, I don't want to throttle your wild enthusiasm," Barclay indicated, "but writing fiction is not just linking and stringing narrative descriptive paragraphs together with good vocabulary, good punctuation and good grammar. Effective fiction writing involves a lot of other ingredients such as author' voice, style, tempo, dialogue, tone, just to name a few," Tom editorialized. "After you've taught that stuff for thirty-five years like I have and analyzed good literature from Twain to Steinbeck, the implementation of those word-smithing techniques comes almost naturally and automatically."

"Well Tom," the dentist alertly interrupted, "I want you to know that I'm both thrilled and delighted at how *you* have deftly *edited* this first story and I'm eager to have you re-edit each of them three more times."

"Well Jim, actually I am more than editing your stories. I'm actually ghost..."

"And Tom!" the ecstatic dentist exclaimed, "I can't wait until you re-edit all twelve of my stories. It's gonna' amount to quite a meritorious collection, I just know it will!"

"Well all right Jim," the more subordinate of the two communicators hesitated and then agreed. "I'll diligently work on several of your other stories and then get motivated to again rewrite 'The Marionette.' I guess the entire twelve-story enterprise could be completed by *New Year's Day*, but don't hold me to that promise in case some snafus pop up in my life."

"Fantastic," the novice author excitedly injected into the phone conversation. "I knew I had selected the right guy to *edit* my work! See ya' soon Tom."

"Okay Jim," Barclay mumbled in a rather confused and disappointed voice. "I'll deliver the stories one at a time to your office and then exchange that new one for a former one already in *your* possession to be rewritten. Your work does show good potential. Good bye Jim."

The retired teacher realized that *he* was going to put forth a "Promethean effort" into "editing" the twelve selections. 'I should've kept my big mouth shut and not have so eagerly volunteered my services,' the man regretfully lamented. 'I could be writing my own collection of short fiction for a hundred percent of the profits and not working just as hard on Dr.

Marshal's crippled novellas for what he describes as a fifteen percent editing fee. I suppose the old adage that stupid people get implicated into stupid situations rings quite true here. I'll just have to chalk this up as a bad experience to avoid repeating.'

For the next three months right through *Christmas* Tom Barclay worked feverishly and incessantly editing, rewriting and ultimately *ghostwriting* Dr. James P. Marshal's twelve novellas until the dozen stories had evolved into sophisticated superb literature. 'These tales would have made classic authors such as *Jack London, Edgar Allan Poe* and *O. Henry* envious. Only one more selection to go,' the former English mentor thought. 'I hope that Jim realizes my invaluable contribution to this endeavor and gives me fifty percent of the royalties and subsidiary rights.'

In the interim from early September to late December, Tom Barclay's ten *Internet* e-books went bonkers, and amazingly, Barclay's pen name Tee Bee Clay became internationally famous. One of *his* works climbed to the lofty *Amazon.com* Sales Ranking of 1,503 out of over three million products listed at the site and the e-book stayed below the highly touted ten thousand mark for over three months. And while Tee Bee Clay's writing reputation was soaring above the literary stratosphere the sensitive man was still obediently honoring his verbal and written commitment and loyally continued ghostwriting Dr. James P. Marshal's twelve mediocre novellas.

Upon delivering the final story "Nom de Plume" to the Egg Harbor City Philadelphia Avenue dentist's office on January 4th of the new year, the two men held a brief conference in the doctor's private office.

"Tom, you've done a really marvelous job editing my twelve manuscripts," the dentist commended, "and I want you to know that I truly value your remarkable *editing* and would recommend you to anyone having designs of becoming an author. You should've gone into newspaper journalism instead of teaching."

"Actually Jim," Tee Bee Clay said, "I really did it as an exclusive favor for you and probably would not have worked so laboriously on the project for anyone else. I really have ghostwritten your work Jim and not edited it as you claim. There's a big difference between editing and ghostwriting, I assure you."

"But Tom, *we* signed a publishing contract, remember?" Dr. Marshal reminded his now-famous editor. "You've already consented to receiving fifteen percent of the proceeds as my official editor. A deal's a deal in my book and if I recollect, we even shook hands on it. Isn't that true?"

"Look Jim!" the now-frustrated Tom Barclay rudely and bluntly intoned, "I'm now a fairly famous author on the *Internet*. Why don't we go fifty-fifty on this novella collection of yours," the disappointed *ghostwriter* suggested. "I have fourteen stories of my own, and *we* could produce two books of stories, thirteen in each. We could then split the money down the middle and then I'll be able to get just compensation for me *ghostwriting* your twelve now-impressive stories!"

"What! You say you want half' interest in my dozen works that I labored two years to create?" the dentist bellowed. "No dice Tom! You're asking too much and violating our contract that quite explicitly states that *you* are entitled to fifteen percent as the editor. Now you want to be co-author and swindle me out of thirty-five percent? No way Jose'!"

"But just be rational for a cotton-pickin' second Jim," Barclay adamantly pleaded. "*Our* two new books will appear listed on *my* ten hot web sites at *Amazon.com, Barnes and Noble, Mobipocket, ebookpalace.com, authorsden.com, Booksamillion, Powell's* among others. You'll sell more books and make more money by being my fifty percent partner in two literary ventures than you will just having your work floating around in cyberspace at a web site or by submitting it to pompous sanctimonious New York City traditional publishing houses. Please reconsider my very fair proposal. Believe me, I know what I'm talking about! A half of a huge loaf of bread is plenty better than eighty-five percent of a tiny loaf. Now that's where I'm coming from!"

"I have reconsidered everything!" the very obstinate amateur writer balked and boomed. "*You* must honor the terms of *our* editing contract Tom and that's final!"

Tom Barclay stormed out of the dentist's office so angrily that he might have committed a deadly felony if he had stayed on the premises and had extended the heated debate. 'I should've known that this sour ending would happen,' he anguished and languished as the indignant fellow swiftly opened the door and entered the driver's side of his mint green *Mazda Protégé* and then quickly slammed it shut in total disgust. 'I made *his* straw into *our* gold, but Marshal doesn't realize that owning a half of a goldmine is far better than owning eighty-five percent of a worthless haystack. I think I know exactly how to fix *his* wagon good! I'll set my plan into motion as soon as I get home.'

Upon arriving at his Buffalo Avenue residence in a disheveled state of mind, Tom had a heart-to-heart discussion with his devoted wife. "Laura, you know I'm not a vindictive person. But I really feel cheated by Jim Marshal," the husband complained. "I've done most of the work on *his* dozen stories and yet *he* still' stubbornly only wants to give me fifteen percent of the royalties. I feel that I'm being used and that he's cunningly pilfered my talent and is capitalizing on my effort by being extremely greedy. I never once suspected *he* would be so avaricious."

"Sometimes it never *pays* to help somebody because you don't know where the relationship is going to lead to," the wife maintained and sympathized. "Tom, you should've never signed that one-sided editing contract with him. Now you're legally bound even though *you* had ghostwritten the stories and not had just edited them as Jim Marshal claims."

"The numskull is so stubborn, so greedy and so inflexible about not giving me my well-deserved just credit and co-authorship in *his* stories," Tom regretfully insisted. "We could've collaborated on future works and jointly shared *their* successes. As you know Laura I'm not a litigious person and despise courtroom lawyers," Barclay told his compassionate wife. "I wasn't brought up that way. But now it looks like there might have to be a judicial settlement to satisfy my grievance."

"I don't think Dr. Marshal realizes exactly how *he* could profit in the future from the ongoing relationship," the Catholic school fourth grade teacher pointed out. "You never really know about someone's character and integrity until money is involved. That is usually the determining factor in any human litmus test! But perhaps Tom we should consider changing dentists. I understand that Dr. Wuillermin over in Hammonton has a good rapport with his clients and a decent reputation too."

Unbeknownst to Jim Marshal, Tom Barclay had shrewdly gone to the *Friendly Copying Shop* in Mays Landing in early December and had spent an entire morning making two photo' copies of all of Dr. James P. Marshal's twelve stories prior to Tom's adroit final editing of the novellas. One copy of each manuscript remained untouched and each was the duplicate of the original that had existed for the dentist's twelve separate registries in the federal government's copyright archives in Washington DC.

After the first major rewrite, Tom had wisely revisited the Mays Landing copying machine retail sales establishment and reproduced facsimiles of the corrected and fully revised work as evidence of *his* intensive labor on Dr. Marshal's "twelve masterpieces." The final fully edited and ghostwritten compositions had been captured on a computer floppy disk and the finished text also existed in Barclay's C-drive as a "Document Word file."

By mid-January the aggrieved author had sufficiently cooled off to be able to finally send his newfound chief nemesis a final protest outlining *his* claim of being co-author of Dr. Marshal's dozen "novella masterpieces." The form and substance of Thomas Eugene Barclay's letter was as follows:

January 15, 2002

Dr. James P. Marshal DDS,

I wholeheartedly regret that you have refused to give me credit and co-authorship in *our* twelve stories. If you recall, I had wished to combine fourteen of my novellas with your twelve tales and produce two stellar collections of admirable literature where we would go 50/50. I truly still believe that I have converted your very mediocre stories into quality word-smithing, yet *you* have ignored my masterful contribution and still maintain that I deserve a meager fifteen-percent editing fee.

I hereby go on record that this letter delivered certified mail will be *Exhibit A* in a forthcoming litigation suit over disputed ownership of the twelve stories beginning with "The Marionette." If *you* attempt publishing the dozen stories without *my* consent, then *your* action will have set the legal process and my steadfast legal protest in motion.

Here is what *you* need to heed Jim, so please fully understand my position and claim:

1) That *my* pen name and/or name (Tee Bee Barclay or Thomas Barclay) is not to appear anywhere on the front cover or inside

your (*our*) published stories. If either my pen name or real name does appear, then I am entitled to fifty percent of royalties and subsidiary rights as the co-author (ghostwriter) and not a mere fifteen-percent pittance portion as "the editor."

2) If my name appears anywhere in *your* book where I am specifically identified as *your* editor, then *you* will be royally sued because my established name in the book marketplace is presently worth and commands a lot more than a lame fifteen percent *editing fee.* You must understand Jim that you stand to gain much more financially by honoring our true relationship in the production of *our* work rather than obstinately and counter-productively arguing that the twelve stories are your exclusive property. The tennis ball is now in your court. I hereby claim that they are now *our* mutual intellectual property because I am your *ghostwriter* and not your *editor.*

3) True, *you* do own the copyrights to *your* original stories, but copyright protection only safeguards your *main ideas* from being published by someone else. Jim, I am not going to publish *our* stories. Please bear in mind that copyright infringement also protects the author's *writing style, writing voice, total text* and *use* of *character dialogue.* Since I have amplified *your* novellas and have rewritten and added at least forty-percent of the current text, I have not just "edited" *your* novellas as you claim. And since *your* stories are written in Tee Bee Barclay's *writing style, writing voice* and *dialogue writing patterns* between characters, and because I have also added great detail, descriptions and narrative to *your* original stories, then I am certainly and definitely their co-author and not just "the editor."

4) If Jim you ignore my protest and publish *your* twelve stories that I have painstakingly *ghostwritten* for *you* then in effect *you* are committing *fraud* by claiming the intellectual property in said stories is eighty-five percent *yours*, when essentially it now is *our* work. This provable fact exists regardless of whether *you* own copyrights to *your* original stories.

5) If you James P. Marshal publish any or all of the twelve stories in bound book form or in e-book format, then the dozen in-question stories must be the exact literature that *you* had

originally produced *before* Thomas Barclay (Tee Bee Barclay) had edited, rewritten and finally ghostwritten said stories for *you,* James P. Marshal.

6) I maintain that I, Thomas E. Barclay have in my possession photo' copies of James P. Marshal's original works and that when compared with the finished products that I had meticulously edited, rewritten and ghostwritten four times each, it can easily be determined and proven in a court of law that I am the co-author. It can also be appropriately evidenced in a court of law that I am the ghostwriter after my attorney simply compares *your* copyrighted documents with *my* finished polished labor on a line-by-line, page-by-page basis.

Jim, I don't like and never have liked litigation. I prefer that we pursue a more reasonable conclusion to this disagreement. I think I have skillfully converted your twelve novellas into "World-class literature." In fact Jim, the truth is that I have worked harder on *your* dozen sci-fi/paranormal stories than you have. You know that just as well as I know that.

If you still plan to go full-speed-ahead without solidifying a 50/50 co-author arrangement with me, then I hereby accuse you of committing literary *fraud* and misrepresentation by attempting to pawn off my name, skill and reputation as being *yours.*

Please reconsider all of these circumstances and ramifications before doing anything drastic on your own. Please be part of the solution instead of being the major part of the problem.

Sincerely,

Thomas Barclay
Tee Bee Barclay (author of ten successful *Internet* books)

The following morning at breakfast Tom was reading the local news in the *Atlantic City Press* when his eyes focused on an article reporting major vandalism done to a familiar Mays Landing copying machine office.

"Laura," the retired English teacher said, "there was extensive vandalism done at the *Friendly Copying Shop* over in Mays

Landing last evening. It's front-page news'! The store's manager says here in the *Press* that the entire place was ransacked and trashed. Eight copying machines had been vandalized and devastated, possibly with a sledgehammer. Total damage is estimated to be around thirty thousand dollars. I sure hope that their business insurance policy covers the expenses."

"Sounds like a major Mafia payback," the wife hypothesized and remarked with a genuine frown on her face. "Say Tom, isn't the *Friendly Copying Shop* where *you* had made duplicate copies of Jim Marshal's manuscripts?"

"You're absolutely right," her husband affirmed showing more than mild interest. "And Manny 'the Beast' Mancuso happens to be Jim Marshal's cousin and close friend. You don't suppose that this was some sort of payback, do you?"

"For letting you make photo' copies of the manuscript, no," Laura disagreed shaking her head, "but for something else like a loan-sharking deal gone sour or failing to pay the mobsters extortion insurance money, yes!"

"Anyway Laura," the wife's sometimes' garrulous spouse lectured, "my copy of the ghostwritten manuscript' is too big to put in *our* safety deposit box at the bank. I'm going to place both the corrected stories and the original unedited copyrighted stories in this portfolio and hide it somewhere. Now to think of the perfect safe place to store it."

"Why not up in the attic?" the wife intelligently and practically suggested.

"No," Tom stated after pondering his self-contrived dilemma for a moment. "I'm going to hide it in mom's attic. No one will think of ransacking *her* place over on St. Louis. I know I'm beginning to sound paranoid but I think that that location would be an intelligent strategic maneuver."

"Tom, I think you're becoming way too neurotic and crazy about this manuscript business involving Jim Marshal," Laura empathetically and confidentially related. "Of course this is all wild speculation Tom, but Manny Mancuso and his Mafia cohorts aren't going to vandalize *our* house looking for the manuscript until those stories are published, selling big and worth something. I'm very certain of that."

"You might be right," the husband reluctantly concurred and then hesitated, "but I can't take that chance. This afternoon I'm taking the portfolio and the copies over to Mom's place and hiding it up in *her* attic."

"I still think you're overreacting to a random news' story," Laura Barclay advised her uptight husband. "The next move is Jim Marshal's ploy in this ongoing mental chess game the two of you are playing," the wife insisted, "and your documents are safe and sound until the doctor tries publishing those stories he claims are only fifteen percent yours."

Later that morning Tom Barclay drove his light green *Mazda Protégé* over to 429 St. Louis Avenue where his widowed mother resided. He knocked on the back screen porch door and then entered the humble abode.

"Hi Mom," Tom greeted with a broad grin. "I've come over to shut the windows up in your attic. Winter has really set in fast and I can't remember if I had closed your attic windows back in November," the son fibbed. "I don't want to see your heating bills suddenly skyrocket and become a little too excessive for your fixed income to handle!"

"You're always thinking of me," Mrs. Ruth Barclay said with a grateful smile on her wrinkled aged countenance. "I'll prepare a cup of coffee for you while you're climbing the pull-down ladder going up to the attic. It should be ready in five minutes. Two sugars and a few drops' of milk as usual."

"Thanks Mom," Tom answered while disguising his neurotic phobia about the portfolio being stolen and about the prospect of his middle-class house on Buffalo Avenue being violated and plundered. "It'll only take me a couple of minutes to check it out and make sure your attic windows are shut!"

After *his* mother walked from the dining room and into her kitchen, Tom stepped onto the back porch, grabbed the aforementioned portfolio off of a dusty card table, opened the door leading from the kitchen to the cellar and then abruptly pulled-down the overhead hinged-ladder. Barclay climbed up the rungs to the attic and then surreptitiously hid the portfolio underneath an old mattress that had been stored there since the early 1970s. After completing his primary mission the devious fellow observed the two already closed attic side-windows as he had promised his mother he would check, carefully descended the rungs, lifted the ladder back into its interior hide-away position and then re-joined his mother in the kitchen. Mrs. Ruth Barclay had already prepared a hot cup of coffee and had sliced some

48

pound cake on a dish and was ready to exchange a little pleasant gossip about cousins, aunts, uncles and Egg Harbor City neighbors.

That January evening Tom and Laura were about to leave *their* house and drive twelve miles west to Hammonton to visit some old *Glassboro State College* friends. Just as they were about to exit the back door, a message came over the couple's police scanner situated on the kitchen counter. "Emergency. Attention: Egg Harbor City Rescue Squad. Go Immediately to 429 St. Louis Avenue. Woman has fallen and is unconscious on lawn outside house. Neighbors called in emergency. Urgent, proceed immediately to home at 429 St. Louis Avenue."

"Oh my God Laura!" Tom exclaimed. "That's Mom they're talking about!"

The two rushed out of their Buffalo Avenue home and Tom recklessly locked the back door. They hopped inside the mint green *Mazda Protégé* and were soon speeding across town to St. Louis Avenue. Upon arriving at their destination the husband and wife noticed a chaotic scene of red blinking lights originating from an ambulance and from local police cars in the street. A woman on a stretcher was being lifted inside the rear compartment of the ambulance parked in the driveway.

Tom and Laura frantically sprinted to the area where the emergency vehicles had been parked. "That's my mother!" Barclay exclaimed. "Has she had a heart attack or stroke?" he yelled over to several rescue squad members.

"That's what we thought at first," the head paramedic said, "but after examining her, we think she's gone into sugar shock. Does your mother have diabetes?"

"Yes she does," Tom anxiously verified. "She's collapsed several times before from the condition. Once I remember was inside *Harrah's Casino* and she had to be rushed to the Atlantic City Medical Center."

"Well," the Egg Harbor City paramedic optimistically said, "we're going to err on the side of caution and transport her over to *Kessler Memorial Hospital* over in Hammonton for total evaluation."

"Ironically, my wife and I were heading over to Hammonton when we heard the call on our police monitor," Tom informed the chief paramedic. "Now we have a more urgent reason for making the trip."

"Okay sir, you can follow the ambulance to Hammonton and reunite with your mom there," the volunteer stated. "We've already contacted *Kessler's* emergency room and they're expecting us. We should be there in fifteen minutes or so."

The volunteer rescue squad members locked the back doors, re-entered their vehicle and then the ambulance slowly backed out of the driveway. Soon it was being followed down the normally quiet residential street by the mint green *Mazda Protégé*. Tom nervously trailed the ambulance (with its red flashing lights) down the remainder of St. Louis Avenue toward busy *Route 30*, the *White Horse Pike*.

"Wait a minute!" Tom yelled to Laura as he' remembered something important. "I'm going to have to turn around and make sure the doors to mom's house are all locked. I don't want any burglars prowling around to have easy access," the very nervous driver said. "Robbers and crooks like Manny Mancuso have police monitors too," the husband anxiously asserted, "and they often rob homes during relatives' funerals and when innocent victims are taken to the hospital!"

"Are you sure you just aren't being overly paranoid about your portfolio being secretly hidden in Mom's attic?" the wife discreetly criticized. "This could be an omen Tom for you to back off and to ease up!"

"I confess I'm a little uptight," Tom hesitantly admitted, "but right now I'm more concerned about robbers burglarizing Mom's property than I am about vandals breaking in and mutilating furniture."

Several minutes later Tom turned around in a *White Horse Pike* driveway and headed three miles back to St. Louis Avenue. Barclay noticed that a fire engine with red blinking lights was seen moving rapidly directly behind the automobile in the green *Mazda's* rear-view mirror. 'I wonder where that's going?' the driver thought. 'This is a very busy street tonight!'

Four blocks further north on St. Louis Avenue Tom and Laura simultaneously spotted smoke and fire rising from the roof of house number 439. The *Protégé'* sped into the driveway and was quickly parked on the rear lawn next to a series of tall rhododendron bushes. The couple hopped out of their' car to better assess the sudden unexpected emergency.

Two Egg Harbor City fire engines promptly stopped on the avenue and the department's men began unwinding hoses to shoot-out jets of water to douse the hungry flames. Scores of neighbors stood on sidewalks in the thirty-two degree temperature to witness the boisterous scene of pandemonium and to crane their necks viewing the ugly damage caused by the spectacular blaze. Police directed the traffic, consisting mostly of rubbernecking ambulance chasers.

"What on earth is going on here?" Tom frantically asked a police officer investigating the fire. "Is this arson? We were just here only minutes ago!"

"Mr. Barclay, after your mother was placed into the ambulance, my partner and I decided to check to make sure all doors to the house had been locked. I then noticed that the back door was unlocked and partially open," an investigating Egg Harbor City patrolman explained. "Apparently your mother had stepped outside, had gone to the utility shed and had fallen on her way back inside. She probably had become unconscious before ever re-entering the house. Those particular details are still sketchy but we're working on them to sort them all out."

"And then," a second conscientious police patrolman interrupted his partner, "when we entered the house we immediately saw smoke and flames coming from the kitchen stove's burners that had apparently ignited the wall. We believe your mother had left a boiling pot on the stove and when the water had evaporated while she was lying unconscious outside," the officer elaborated, "a spark must have ignited a napkin or something else flammable, and then a flash fire broke out while your mom was being taken to Kessler Hospital."

After being consoled by Laura, Tom approached the city's fire chief for an accurate assessment of the damages. The beleaguered man didn't like what he heard.

"Sorry to report to you Mr. Barlcay," the chief began in a sympathetic voice, "but the entire roof and all property in the attic have been completely destroyed in the inferno. There's nothing up there that can be salvaged, so be prepared to make out a list of items that were stored up there for insurance claims' purposes," the fire official stated as hoses continued splashing torrents of water onto the house's roof and into the badly charred open attic holes. "There'll be plenty of water damage too!" the chief grimly informed his distraught listener.

On the drive east to Hammonton's *Kessler Memorial Hospital* Tom and Laura Barclay conducted a rather frank conversation.

The man had become both shocked and dismayed at the bizarre sequence of out-of-control events that had recently developed and that had completely marred his tumultuous day. He sought consolation from his devoted wife.

"I now know I should've hidden that lousy portfolio in the cellar rather than stashing it in the attic of Mom's house," the thoroughly unnerved driver maintained on his way west on the *White Horse Pike* to Hammonton. "Sometimes being too conscientious is a person's worst enemy, wouldn't you agree? Now tell me Laura, what do you think about all of this horrible stinkin' bad luck skein I've experienced today?"

"I hate to criticize your judgment or your priorities," the wife diplomatically began, "but the portfolio would've been safer sitting on the kitchen' table in our own house. But in all fairness," Laura continued, "hindsight always has better vision than does foresight. And unfortunately, neither of us is clairvoyant. But your primary concern right now should be your mother's condition, don't you agree?"

"Well yes it should, but now Laura we don't have to worry any longer about Manny 'the Beast' Mancuso and his *Mafia* associates discovering the photo' copied twelve manuscripts because they've been incinerated in the attic inferno," Tom disgustedly sulked while also grieving about his mother's close call with almost freezing to death while lying unconscious on her side lawn. And then Barclay considered his mother's subsequent fire emergency, which she had yet to learn about.

"It's a good thing mother has newsy nosy neighbors that saw her sprawled-out on the ground in mid-winter temperature," Laura perceptively commented. "The dual tragedies could've been a lot worse if the Baldwins' had been away on vacation." The wife paused for a moment to clear her somewhat cluttered mind. "And I just remembered Tom, you still have Jim Marshal's finished disks and his polished manuscripts on your computer's hard-drive."

"As usual, you're right Laura," the now-famous *Internet* novelist/novellas writer agreed. "And after I get copies of the original texts from the federal government's copyright office, then I can still prove that I had contributed just as much to covetous Jim Marshal's finished literature as he had."

"Sometimes when *you* become too overly-concerned about what could or might happen," Laura Barclay fathomed and

52

explained, "then your haste and apprehension make *you* lose control of what actually *does* happen. Tom, your greatest fear became a sort of self-fulfilling prophecy!"

"Youth Revisited"

One August 2001 Monday morning Frederick Richard Barker drove his sky-blue *Buick LeSabre* east on busy *Route 30* to the *Blueberry Crossing Shopping Center*. The retired Hammonton, New Jersey brick and stone mason was a seventy-year-old health fanatic that was fighting a valiant battle against the onslaught of everyone's common nemesis, old age. Fred parked his recently washed automobile in a convenient space and then strolled from the asphalt onto the pavement into the *Health Tree Nutrition Store* to purchase a re-supply of Vitamin E and a new bottle of potent *Multi-Vitamins and Minerals*.

"Hi," Fred politely addressed the preoccupied young girl standing behind the counter taking care of a demanding customer. "Where's Sharon? She usually takes good care of me."

"Mrs. Bertino is in New York attending a health products trade show," the conscientious girl answered as she was ringing up the fastidious customer's acquisitions on the cash register. "She'll be back in town on Wednesday unless she begins that *Pocono Mountains* vacation she's been talking about."

"Thanks for the info'," the regular patron replied with a forced smile. "Where's Bill, the manager? He always knows exactly what I need."

"Oh," the pretty blonde teenaged employee said, "Bill had complained that he's gotten another expensive speeding ticket and right now he's over at Town Hall paying the fine. He's worried about losing his license."

"Yeah, that makes a lot of sense," Fred answered. "He's always buzzing around in that new red sports car of his. I guess that's what happens when you take too many vitamins," the twice a month *Health Tree* visitor joked. "All that energy must go directly to *your* right foot. Maybe Billy the Kid can bribe the cop with a few bottles of cholesterol tablets designed specifically for chronic coffee drinkers and doughnut munchers."

The pleasant young lady smiled in response to Fred's jovial demeanor and mild sarcasm and then focused her attention on another customer's nutritional needs. Fred Barker sauntered over to a retail display rack and instinctively selected the two familiar bottles of vitamins and minerals he was in quest of. Then the health store patron stepped to the main counter and placed the items next to the cash register. The fresh-out-of-high-school employee was a bit overwhelmed and flustered simultaneously waiting on two customers while nervously explaining to a third her mantra about where Sharon and Bill were.

Fred Barker then remembered he had only a half bottle of *Cava Cava* left on the kitchen counter at home, so he figured he would try and locate it himself until the pressured rookie store attendant could get caught up on *her* challenging sales' responsibilities. For several minutes Barker systematically searched the display racks to no avail, concluded that the *Health Tree* had sold out of that particular product, theorized that the girl behind the counter was unfamiliar with the retail outlet's inventory and then, resigned to failure, returned to the vicinity of the cash register. The attractive-but-impulsive novice cashier already had Fred's two acquisitions totaled up and tucked inside a plastic bag.

"Anything else sir?" the freckle-faced young lady courteously inquired. "I'm trying to get caught up with sales. I usually handle the stock room inventory and just occasionally work up here helping people during an emergency."

"I was looking for some *Cava Cava* but I guess I'll buy it next time around when either Sharon or Bill happens to be here," the purchaser casually remarked. "I still have half a bottle of the stuff at home that should tide me over until the next time I'm in the vicinity."

"Thank you sir," the clerk sincerely stated. "Bill said I wouldn't be rushed when he left the store, and then around twenty customers have come in and bought vitamins and health foods in the last fifteen minutes. I'm still trying to figure out all of the special discount keys on the cash register!"

"That's okay, I understand perfectly," the retired man calmly said. "You'll catch on in a hurry. Just charge me for the two bottles I had placed on the counter. I'll buy the *Cava Cava* in two weeks when my supply runs out. Like I said, I still have half a bottle remaining at home."

"*Cava Cava*," the girl laughed. "That's my favorite rock band. I didn't know it was a health product too! I learn a lot of interesting things working here!"

"It's very good for calming the nerves and soothing one's restless spirit," Fred patiently explained to the *Health Tree* apprentice. "When you're my age young lady, you'll know that you need to stay relaxed. I'm trying to outdistance the *Grim Reaper* and his buddies who are in hot pursuit on my trail! It's a futile struggle we all lose in the end, ya' know!"

"Sir, that'll be $22.95," the blushing self-conscious girl announced. "Thank you for your consideration during my minor trauma!"

Fred amiably paid the prescribed total and then ambled out of the busy store holding the glass door open for some more clientele who were eagerly entering the *Health Tree*. Barker drove home smiling, wishing that he were seventeen again and charming enough at that pristine age to ask the pretty *Health Tree* girl for a date. "Time passes more swiftly than we humans realize," Barker said to his wrinkled face in the *LeSabre's* rear-view mirror. "Where have all these years gone?" he mildly complained to his aged reflection as a traffic light at the intersection of Broadway and *Route 30* switched to green. "We're all vulnerable to the advance of time no matter what kind of physical shape we're in! I'm just trying to cheat Mother Nature out of a few additional years, that's all!"

Upon returning to his well-maintained Peach Street red-brick rancher Fred was disappointed when he opened the plastic bag on the kitchen table and examined his purchases. The Vitamin E bottle was the same as the one he had selected from the shelf but the Multi-Vitamin and Mineral purchase was definitely not the same package Barker had chosen.

'The young girl must have gotten my sale mixed up with another customer's order when I had gone to the back of the store looking for *Cava Cava*,' the rational fellow immediately suspected. 'I should have known that she was inexperienced and working under duress. Instead I stupidly tried flirting with her when I'm old enough to be her great-grandfather,' Barker regretfully thought while simultaneously shaking his head and smiling about *his* own shallow vanity.

The disappointed man removed the Multi-Vitamin and Mineral bottle from its outer packaging and carefully inspected its unique label. '120 tablets. Take one daily every morning. Guaranteed to make you *feel* more youthful,' he skeptically read. 'Manufactured by the *Eternal Youth Corporation*, Young,

Arizona.' Then Fred reflected for a moment and generalized, 'This product sounds like some sort of rip-off to me!'

Intrigued by the plastic bottle's label, Fred paced to his den and removed *World Book Encyclopedia A* from a dusty bookshelf. Much to Barker's amusement his curiosity and his research discovered that a place named Young, Arizona actually existed in the center of the state, and interestingly enough, it had no population statistic provided in the encyclopedia.

'Probably a fraudulent ghost town without a bona fide *Zip Code* too,' the man mused as he returned the encyclopedia back to its proper place. 'But I'm so fascinated by the claims of these *Multi-Vitamin and Mineral* tablets that I'll give them a try,' the "health-freak" decided. 'It also says on the label *'For Men Only'*. Now that's a laugh and a half,' Barker cynically imagined. 'We even have specialized vitamins and minerals for each gender. Now I really suspect that those tablets in that ordinary-looking brown plastic bottle are a real scam.'

Fred swallowed down a Multi-Vitamin and Mineral capsule every morning for several weeks and soon forgot about the peculiar coincidence between Young, Arizona and *Eternity Youth Products, Inc.* The elderly but still muscular fellow soon noticed the gray areas of his hair disappearing amidst expanding black hair growth and he also happily observed the regions of his male pattern baldness thickening and regaining a healthy and full youthful texture. 'I no longer see the overhead bathroom light reflecting off my scalp,' the astonished man realized.

The structural tissue of Fred Barker's biceps, shoulders and arms began exhibiting vernal muscular definition, fat was rapidly vanishing from his midriff and telltale old age wrinkles were being replaced by smooth skin all over his streamlined body.

"This product is absolutely miraculous!" an exhilarated Fred Barker told Sharon Bertino over the telephone a week later while marveling at the terrific results. "I want to order a whole case of it if you have the item in stock! Whatever ingredients are in those tablets are awfully effective. I haven't felt and looked this swell in over thirty years."

"But the name you've provided me with, 'Multi-Vitamin and Mineral Formula from *Eternal Youth, Corporation* is nowhere in the *Health Tree's* extensive inventory," the confused store-owner answered in a rather uncharacteristic puzzled tone of voice. "I'm now checking my computer database and there's no evidence of any such product anywhere," Sharon conveyed to her disbelieving listener. "Fred, please look on the bottle and see if a *Health Tree* price stamp is on there. Maybe this item can be traced that way. Can you do me that favor?"

"Actually Sharon," Barker authoritatively said, "the sticker on the bottle reads $12.95 but it's just a typical-looking pink label with the cost typed on it, but the label isn't green and it doesn't officially read the words *Health Tree* on it!"

"That's very strange indeed," Sharon Bertino commented to her caller. "This sounds like some sort of prank and you're the unwary victim by purchasing the vitamins by accident," Sharon speculated and revealed. "If you'd like Fred you can bring the vitamin and mineral bottle back to the store and I'll give you a full refund," the proprietor stated in a slightly embarrassed tone of voice. "We have a record that you obtained the item here."

"That's perfectly all right Sharon," Fred optimistically remarked. "I'll take my chances with this sensational product," the happy retired mason vociferated as he proudly admired his vernal appearance in the den mirror over the fireplace mantel. "I have a four month supply so see if you can locate a distributor that handles this remarkable item," Barker requested. "I'll take out a loan and buy a fifty-year supply if I have to."

"Okay, I know you're exaggerating but I'll thoroughly investigate the matter," the somewhat perplexed proprietor returned. "But I assure you Fred, I've been in this business for over twenty years and I've never heard of such a company as *Eternity Youth Products, Incorporated* of Young, Arizona."

"All right Sharon, just keep me posted on your progress or lack thereof," the bewildered caller demanded. "Maybe it's psychological or mind-over-matter," the retired mason claimed, "but quite truthfully I have complete faith and confidence in this wonderful product I'm now taking."

A full month elapsed and Fred Barker was soundly conquering the persistent nemesis commonly known to all humans as "the aging process.' 'Now I can temporarily put the hospital geriatrics ward on hold,' Fred imaginatively thought and grinned, 'and I won't need the services of a wheelchair or oxygen tank for at least fifty more years if I can get my hands on more of these tremendous tablets. And with my insight, experience and maturity,' Fred further whimsically pondered, 'I could avoid the social and peer pressure problems of the younger generation and besides that, I'll have no major financial obligations now that the first and second mortgages on the house have been satisfied.'

The affable retired tradesman climbed into his *Buick LeSabre* and drove over to *A.T. Auto Clinic* on the corner of Fairview Avenue and *Route 30* to honor the car's next scheduled three-thousand-mile servicing and oil change.

"Gee Mr. Barker," Anthony (one of the brother co-owners of the auto' clinic) began, "you're looking much younger than you did the last time I saw you. Are you dyeing your hair? It's hard to keep a thing like that a secret with all of the snoopy people around this town perpetually gossiping non-stop day and night!"

"Anthony, thanks a lot for the sincere compliment," Fred gratefully acknowledged. "For some peculiar reason, I do feel more masculine and more virulent than I ordinarily do. Maybe I'm entering my second childhood or catching my second wind, or something weird like that!"

"You almost look like a college student," Lou (the other mechanic on duty at the auto clinic) interrupted. "Fred, I can't believe how youthful you look," Anthony's younger brother said. "I'll bet a lot of eligible single women and widows you know are keeping tabs on you."

"Tell you the truth Louie," Fred communicated with a broad smile, "I do notice a certain sparkle in their eyes when they say 'hello' to me now. It's almost like I'm some sort of *Hollywood* celebrity or someone special like that! Or, it might just be my wild imagination at work."

"Have you discovered what that guy *Ponce de Leon* was searching for?" Anthony butted in' as was his bad habit. "You know Fred, that legendary Florida *Fountain of Youth* thing we studied about in school?"

"Well Tony, sort of," Fred Barker answered after clearing his throat. "Maybe I'm going through puberty for the second time around. It just might be an extraordinary case of glandular revitalization or something strange like that! I'm happy as long as I believe I'm getting younger and not older."

"When ya' finally find out exactly what it is," Lou insisted, "bottle the secret formula' and sell some to me. I feel like I'm eighty already and I'm still fifteen years away from receiving my first *Social Security* benefits!"

After leaving *A.T. Auto Clinic* Fred drove east on *Route 30* to *Dunkin' Donuts*. Betty Martin, a seventy-year-old 1949

Hammonton High School classmate and former Hammonton High School prom queen was standing in line directly behind Fred at the main counter, waiting to be served.

"Why Fred Barker!" Betty ecstatically exclaimed. "My word, I haven't seen you in years. Ten years since our last reunion," Betty continued as she admired her former heartthrob, "and all of our former teachers are now planted in the cemetery. But you," Betty Martin said in more-than-mild astonishment, "you look like you haven't aged since we dated during the *Vietnam War* back in the early '70s. How have you managed to cheat the daily assault of the aging process?"

"Oh hi Betty," Fred nonchalantly said when he finally recognized the identity of his longtime admirer. "I attribute it all to clean healthy living, laying off of tobacco and alcohol, and also to drinking three tall glasses of milk and three double glasses of water daily. That's been my strategy for combating my dreaded admission into the geriatrics ward."

"Anything else?" the formerly beautiful woman anxiously asked. "I have a bit of vanity left in me too!"

The doughnut purchaser stared directly into Betty's pathetic-looking eyes and then gazed at her wrinkled countenance. "Yes Betty," Fred fabricated, "I also believe in sleeping and eating and going to the bathroom at the exact same times every day and practicing yoga breathing exercises and *Transcendental Meditation*!" he facetiously stated.

"I'll have to try doing those things you've suggested," Betty agreed, "because the results you've obtained are absolutely convincing evidence to me. Forgive my frankness," Betty Martin proceeded and confided, "but you're probably the most talked about and sought after seventy-year-old man in all of Hammonton, and I mean that as honest-to-God truth!"

"You're very kind and I'm quite flattered," Fred said while winking at his female acquaintance with a twinkle in his left eye. The man received his three double-chocolate doughnuts from the dark-complexioned foreign woman attendant and then haughtily paced out of the popular junk-food establishment.

Later in the day the retired mason had ordered a "small pizza with extra-thick crust and extra cheese" from *Bruni's Pizzeria* on Twelfth Street. Sam, the owner of the place, praised Fred on his youthful appearance.

"Mr. Barker," Sam said as he paused from kneading dough and then flipping the rounded mass into the air, "you're looking more and more like *Hercules* every day. And your hair is no longer salt and pepper. How do ya' manage to keep yourself in such incredible shape?"

"Sam, please don't say that," the pizza purchaser blandly balked. "I'm a student of mythology and I wholeheartedly assure you that *Hercules* has been dead for over three thousand years! I plan to be around for at least two decades more!"

"Regardless," the pizza expert persisted, "how have you managed to recapture your youth? Are you some sort of sorcerer or alchemist?"

"Oh Sam!" Fred chuckled, "I just believe that a healthy mind and a strong body go hand-in-hand," the retired brick and stone contractor said, inadvertently quoting the ancient Greek scholar *Plato*. "Take care of yourself, eat three square meals a day including plenty of Bruni's pizza, and don't watch annoying television soap operas. And oh yes, stay away from ugly women! That's the essence of my successful reclusive lifestyle."

"I'll have to remember that sage advice," Sam acceded in sheer wonderment. "If I can look like you do right now, I'd be the envy of every pizzeria owner in New Jersey. I'd even join a monastery if I had to!" Sam said as the owner's wife shook her head in disgust.

That night after consuming his small tomato and cheese pie Fred reviewed the significant details of his mediocre life. Children Jeff and Jill were each happily married, the son living with *his* wife in San Diego and the daughter a single professional real estate/stock broker residing in Manhattan. Wife Dottie had contracted breast cancer in the late 1980s and succumbed to the insidious disease in February of 1995. Barker was now free to find another woman, and since his seventy-year-old body had now been replenished and restored to one belonging to a thirty-year-old male stud, the retired mason was ready to again go hunting for a suitable mate in the wild and crazy social jungle.

'I long for female companionship,' the man admitted to his now clear conscience. 'I'll try my luck at romance at the gaming tables over in Atlantic City and see exactly what *Lady Luck* has in store for me. Life and love are just as much dangerous gambles as roulette wheels are,' Fred Barker aptly concluded. 'And if Atlantic City falls through there's always Las Vegas.'

The following Saturday night Fred decided that he was adequately prepared to venture out on "woman scouting patrol" at *Harrah's Casino* on the northern boundary of Atlantic City bordering the family resort town of Brigantine. 'I remember taking Dottie to the boardwalk back in the early '50s, eating salt water taffy, and going to dances on the *Steel Pier*,' Fred recalled as he motored eastward on *Route 30* in his sky metallic blue *Buick LeSabre.* 'My God! How things have changed since the fabulous 1950s! Who would have ever thought that casino gambling would resurrect Atlantic City back into the '*Queen of Resorts.* Wildwood, Ocean City, Cape May and Seaside Heights have to really struggle to try and keep up!'

Barker piloted his *Buick* off of the *White Horse Pike* and soon was heading up Brigantine Boulevard past the opulent *Borgata Casino Hotel* and the *Trump Marina* towards *Harrah's.* The glitter and excitement of the hectic casino filled the driver's mind with anticipation as he turned the steering wheel in the direction of the hotel's newly remodeled valet parking area.

After entrusting his nondescript vehicle to a nondescript casino attendant, Fred Barker entered the flamboyant world of chance, gamble and romance. The man's pulse increased as he boldly strode inside, his feet keeping a cadence to the rhythm of a '50s rock and roll tune blaring from *Harrah's Casino's* twenty-four-hour non-stop background music system amidst the clanging of bells, buzzers and coins falling from slot machine tumblers and being deposited into deep metal trays.

'I'll try my hand at the blackjack table first,' Fred thought. 'The odds are much better there than at the money-hungry slot machines. And besides, I can sit down and hopefully a beautiful woman will suddenly appear like magic in the seat next to me,' he imaginatively daydreamed even though it was nighttime.

The robust casino visitor walked past several active roulette wheel counters and then conveniently stationed himself in a comfortable black leather chair at a poker table. A swarthy-skinned attractive Polynesian doll was the dealer at the ten-dollar minimum per game table.

Fred's luck was mediocre for the first half-hour, playing the house even. Then his fortunes changed for the better when a knockout blonde approached and swiftly sat in the seat to Barker's right. Soon the energized man struck-up a friendly conversation with the gorgeous bombshell.

"Hi," Barker instinctively greeted the fantastically built alluring young lady. "Are you a cover girl or a model?" he praised. "You certainly look like one!"

"Hardly!" the woman replied while checking out Fred's stellar build and handsome face. "I'm just a school teacher from Ventnor trying my luck at poker. I got a little lonesome tonight so I figured I'd give *Harrah's* a whirl."

"Well, my name's Fred Barker," the excited man said with a serious blush' evident on his cheeks. "Can I buy you a drink? What's your pleasure?" the gambler said as a free-drink scantily clad attendant came sauntering by with her empty tray.

"Yes, a pina colada would be just fine," the luscious blonde declared while waiting for the beverage server to come around to their location. "My name's Jessica Hughs. I'm a widow. My husband died in a terrible automobile accident four years ago this very night."

"That's really too bad," Fred Barker answered in a feigned sympathetic voice that satisfactorily camouflaged his overall delight at his new acquaintance being unattached. "My wife Dottie died of breast cancer a while back and I haven't quite gotten over the shock yet. It's a difficult and lonely existence once *you're* used to being married and then suddenly find yourself jolted into isolation. Stark reality can be quite discouraging at times. Wouldn't you agree Jessica?"

"I know exactly what you mean," Jessica Hughs readily admitted. "It hasn't been easy for me either. Loneliness can become a self-destructive torture!"

"Are you Scandinavian?" Fred perceptively asked as he glanced at Jessica's fair skin. "You look exactly like that blonde chick that used to sing in the Swedish group *ABBA*. Agnetha was her name, I think!"

"Very astute of you to make *that* observation," Jessica bashfully stated and complimented. "Not about the name Agnetha, but about me being Scandinavian. My maiden name was Olson, and my parents were both Swedish immigrants. So, I suppose that now my real name again is Jessica Olson although I still officially go by Jessica Hughs."

The formerly preoccupied friendly cocktail attendant finally wiggled her way over to the poker table to take orders. "Give us a pina colada and a scotch on the rocks," Fred assertively declared to the well-proportioned lady clad in a skimpy cocktail waitress outfit. "And please have the bartender make the drinks extra-large. Here's a twenty dollar tip for your cooperation."

"Why thank you sir!" the cocktail waitress gratefully exclaimed. "Since the drinks are on the house the bartender will surely fix your orders to your specifications after I tell him how generous your tip was! Incidentally, the bartender's my husband and he'll get ten bucks of this twenty!"

Fred and Jessica were compatible right from the very start, and the two were quite jovial after losing two hundred dollars each at the blackjack table. After four rounds of drinks the half-inebriated twosome left the boisterous casino area and wove their way through a throng of people, finally finding sanctuary in a main lobby cocktail lounge where they chatted and listened to oldies' song lyrics performed by a talented *Elvis* impersonator. Soon their romance was flourishing.

"You know Fred," Jessica earnestly said as she sipped her fifth pina colada," I really wish I had lived back in the more sedate 1950s. It seems like such an innocent decade from various movies I've seen and from the songs of that era before the widespread use of drugs and before kids were exposed to sexually transmitted lethal diseases like AIDS."

"I know where you're coming from," the blonde's newfound escort agreed. "I've often wished the exact same thing. I've always dreamed about going to *American Bandstand* and about slow dancing at sock hops!"

"Kids back then seemed more honest and sincere," Jessica astutely added, "and they had more respect for family, for country and for American traditions."

"You're absolutely right," Fred concurred. "It was a very special era where people were more genuine, more civilized, more human! I mean," Fred rambled and slurred on despite his addled mind, "I mean to say Jessica, that's what I've also concluded by watching old movies, by seeing *Ozzie and Harriet* TV reruns and by listening to the style of music from that incomparable time period."

The two were now most attracted to one another. At first it was a renewal in their hearts of the strong animal magnetism that is associated with "love at first sight" but soon there was a melding of kindred spirits and the definite presence of a powerful emotional connection. This was the resurfacing of vital important feelings that both had longed for since the deaths of their spouses.

Now that fervor for opposite-sex companionship had ironically been rekindled by a random chance encounter.

"How about a date?" Fred candidly proposed. "And please, 'Don't Be Cruel'!" the half-intoxicated fellow clarified as he alluded to and then mimicked the lyrics of the *Elvis* tune being sung twenty-feet-away by the suave side-burned impersonator.

"You Ain't Nothin' But a Hound Dog!" the slightly bombed blonde bombshell merrily reacted. "You Can 'Be My Teddy Bear'!" Jessica cleverly and creatively improvised. "How could I possibly resist your advances?"

The first gourmet restaurant date led to a second and in a matter of a month, the pair was having an intense love affair. Fred would stay four nights at Jessica's place ideally situated on a Ventnor beach block and the gorgeous Swedish doll would reciprocate by spending the rest of the week at Fred's cozy and secluded Hammonton abode. Each love session became more intense than its predecessor and the passionate pair openly shared years of suppressed feelings in the form of lovemaking and mutual affection.

The Friday before Palm Sunday Fred surprised Jessica with his announcement of an April vacation to Las Vegas. "I've booked a *United* flight out of Philly' for six nights at *New York, New York*," the euphoric man told his totally elated new soul mate. "Jessie, have your bags packed for a Monday flight departing from *Concourse C.* We're gonna' paint the town red and every other color of the rainbow too! Be prepared for the time of your life. And of course Jessie, I'm treatin' and payin' all the expenses."

"What great timing!" Jessica enthusiastically noted. "It's the week of Easter vacation, well, we teachers call it Spring Break now, and I won't miss a day of school!"

The new lovers' smooth flight arrived without a hitch at Las Vegas *McCarran International Airport* and then the two "almost newlyweds" removed their four suitcases from an airport rotary carousel and were soon transported by a hotel shuttle transfer service to 3790 Las Vegas Boulevard, the dazzling *New York, New York Hotel and Casino.*

"Wow! Look at that replica *Statue of Liberty,* the authentic-looking New York City fire-boat in the water and the magnificent skyscraper façade!" Jessica verbally marveled. "It's almost like being in the *Big Apple* way out here in the Nevada desert!"

66

"And don't forget that scale-model rendition of the *Brooklyn Bridge* walkway decorating the front of the hotel," Fred merrily added. "This whole adult fantasy world Jessie is like a wonderful dream come true!"

"I read in the flight magazine on our *United Air* jet that the casino is designed to give the appearance of *O. Henry's* New York. Everything is fashioned as if it were 1890 again," the excited blonde revealed. "Even the restaurants, the sidewalk cafes, the reproduced *Central Park* setting and the really unique retail stores reflect the 1890s' theme."

"And I had read in a brochure that *New York, New York* has scale models of a *Central Park* bridge, 1890s' *Time Square* and *Greenwich Village* homes and shops all as part of the general casino atmosphere. I'm glad I had booked this place for our memorable Las Vegas vacation!" Jessica's newfound escort exclaimed. "I find the whole place rather invigorating!"

"Tell me, are there any other specific casinos you'd like to visit after our first few days at *New York, New York*?" Jessica asked.

"Yes, as a matter of fact there are," Fred answered rather emphatically. "Several buddies back in Hammonton told me that *Binions Casino* in Old Downtown Las Vegas has the best steaks and prime rib dishes in the world. *Binions* is a must toward the end of our Nevada hiatus."

After checking in at the stately *New York, New York* "mahogany-paneled Registration Desk," a bellhop led the couple over to the elevator lobby. "This incredible place even has an active *Coney Island*-style roller coaster circling it!" Fred stated as the three entered the lobby-level elevator. The helpful bellhop quickly pressed the button for the tenth floor. "After we unpack our things we'll have to investigate all of the sights in this hotel and then we'll tour some of the other palaces and castles on the glitzy 'strip' after tonight," Barker suggested to Jessica.

"You're so well-organized," Jessica Hughs answered as the elevator doors finally slammed shut. "I knew I was immediately attracted to you for some obvious reason!" she said as the accommodating bellboy raised his eyebrows wishing that he were Fred.

The first evening in the glittering fantasy-land was spent touring the *New York, New York* premises. The pair enjoyed having supper at *Gallagher's Steak House*, seeing the fantastic stage-show "Lord of the Dance" in the thousand-seat *Broadway*

Theater and then casually strolling along the simulated boardwalk in the authentic-looking *Coney Island Pavilion.* Finally the New Jersey couple unsuccessfully experimented "unproven gambling theories" with several games of chance inside the enormous casino.

"It's as if we're both kids again," Fred declared. Barker had never been completely frank with Jessica, keeping his true age a secret and pretending that he was a robust and ambitious thirty-five-year-old prominent brick and stone mason that had recently sold his business.

"If that's the case, I hope we both remain kids for the rest of our lives!" Barker's new soul mate bantered back. "If only we could freeze this week in time!"

"Maybe some day a clever scientist will invent a formula that'll allow us to live to be two hundred wonderful years, our lives full of youthful vim and vigor," Fred deliberately conjectured and shared. "Anything's possible nowadays you know thanks to the modern marvels of science and research!"

"Yes, I really hope so," Jessica attested, "because I haven't felt so enthusiastic and so thrilled about something since I was an eager bright-eyed teenager exploring the many sights of the *Atlantic City Boardwalk* for the first time."

On Tuesday the couple toured the main attractions of the Las Vegas strip, visiting such magnificent edifices as the *Bellagio,* the *Mirage,* the *Venetian* and the *Treasure Island* hotels and casinos. Jessica and Fred had used up two rolls of film just capturing the volcanic eruptions outside the *Mirage* along with the entrancing dancing fountains that were situated near the front gardens of the majestic and palatial *Bellagio.*

"I really enjoyed the pirate battle outside *Treasure Island,*" Fred confessed. "It's as if I was a twelve-year-old freckle and acne-faced kid again," Barker confessed to his new soul mate. "I always wanted to be a buccaneer when I was a kid but soon changed my impractical ambition of being a swashbuckling pirate to desiring to play baseball for the *Phillies* when I was ten."

"I want you to promise me that we'll return to Las Vegas at least once every five years," Jessica insisted as she wrapped her arms around Barker's slim waist and gave him a peck on the cheek in front of the *Venetian's* simulated *Campanile* clock tower. "This whole place is an absolute adult fantasy world come true and I want to sincerely thank you for booking it."

"You have my word of honor that we'll return here again and again," Fred promised. "I love Vegas because there are no clocks in the casinos and time seems to stand still, or for that matter Jessie," Barker elaborated, "time seems completely irrelevant and unimportant wherever we decide to roam in this magical concrete and neon paradise."

The couple discussed touring downtown Fremont Street later in the week and viewing the fantastic laser light show projected hourly onto an overhead domed screen serving as an outdoor pavilion for tourists. And the original familiar old time casinos were an alluring attraction when the spectacular colorful nighttime laser light presentations were not in progress.

"Several blocks of Fremont Street have been closed off to allow for a mall-like pedestrian atmosphere," Fred informed Jessica, "and according to a pamphlet I had picked up in the *New York, New York* lobby, the phenomenal nighttime laser show features cartoon characters dancing to *Motown* songs and jet fighter planes flying the length of the three-block-long screen with accompanying authentic sound simulation."

"And don't forget about your juicy steak at *Binions Casino*," Jessica reminded Barker. "I understand that the whole downtown section of the old original casinos has been revitalized, just like our spirits have been rejuvenated!"

On Tuesday the couple booked a tourist bus trip out to *Hoover Dam* and were thoroughly impressed by the gigantic man-made wonder, even taking an underground tour to inspect the subterranean operations of the colossal hydro-electric producing generators. Upon returning to the surface, the lovers discussed the magnificence of picturesque *Lake Mead*.

"It's hard to believe that something so majestic has been man-made by *Hoover Dam* harnessing the power of the mighty Colorado River," Barker related to Jessica.

"And all of this mammoth construction was admirably accomplished during the *Great Depression* before men had advanced technology and specially-designed-equipment," Jessica Olson Hughs concluded and related as their tour bus passed through Henderson on the trip back to Vegas.

Another highlight of the week-long vacation came on Wednesday when Fred rented a car and the two adventurers motored out to the *Painted Desert* where they gazed at and photographed the splendor and the beauty of colorful rock formations and "raw nature."

"You don't see anything like this back in Jersey," Jessica observed and stated. "It's a completely refreshing environment that we're experiencing. No pinelands, boardwalks or beaches anywhere. It seems Fred that civilization and chaos miraculously ends a mile or so outside Vegas."

"True Jessie," her traveling companion amiably agreed. "It's as if we're the only two people left in the whole-wide-world and finally appreciating its total magnificence. It's like this is *Genesis* and we're Adam and Eve reincarnated!"

"That's a very poetic and romantic analogy," Jessica keenly indicated. "One of your literary ancestors must have been *William Shakespeare.*"

On Thursday morning Fred and Jessica had breakfast in a classic-themed restaurant inside *Caesar's Palace* and then did some light souvenir shopping in the casino-hotel's gigantic mall, which featured impressive talking statues of gods from Roman mythology. The fascinated visitors especially delighted in hearing *Bacchus's* raucous monologue.

"*Bacchus* was the Roman god of wine, a real strange character who lived exclusively for pleasure," Fred informed his spellbound traveling partner, "and the Romans borrowed the idea of *Bacchus* from *Dionysus,* the Greek god of wine and merriment."

"You really know your Greek and Roman mythology," Jessie admitted. "You could have been a dynamic ancient history professor if you wanted to be!"

Somewhat exhausted from the week's accumulative escapades, the pair finally trekked back to *New York, New York* to relax and unwind. Jessica desired to don a bikini and sip a tasty pina colada by the hotel's pool but Fred preferred to "take a serious nap" and then join his female companion at poolside in "about two hours."

"Is tonight still on in Old Downtown Las Vegas?" Jessica asked. "I can't wait to go there again!"

"Certainly is," Fred affirmatively replied. "I'm anxious to once again feast on that giant prime rib over at *Binions*. It's gotta' be the highlight of our trip, I just know it! I can almost taste that juicy prime rib' platter right now! And we just gotta' have a repeat performance of that dazzling sound and light display that's shown outside the casinos."

After Jessie left the tenth-floor air-conditioned room for her free outdoor "tanning seminar," Fred was smitten with temporary curiosity. 'Jessie took a twenty dollar bill to buy two pina colidas,' Fred recalled, 'so now's my chance to inspect her wallet, find her driver's license and learn exactly how old *she* really is,' Barker impulsively contemplated.

The man rummaged through the top left drawer of Jessica's bureau and soon located the object of his impetuous quest. He quickly removed her pocketbook and after a minute of frantic fumbling, found her New Jersey driver's license. His eyes nearly popped out of their sockets when his hungry pupils closely scrutinized her date of birth.

'My God!' Fred imagined. 'October 9th, 1931! Jessica is a month older than I am!' the youthful-looking man astonishingly realized about his similarly revitalized partner.

Then a brown paper bag inside the top left bureau drawer caught the rummager's attention. Inside was a bottle of Multi-Vitamins and Minerals that surprisingly had been manufactured by the aforementioned *Eternal Youth Corporation* of Young, Arizona. The stunned man quickly unscrewed the cap and noticed that Jessica's bottle was two-thirds full.

'I only have about a thirty-day supply left,' Fred avariciously estimated. 'I'll cheat a little bit and take one of her capsules right now and then transfer five more to my bottle so that I can extend my happy flirtation with youth revisited.'

The man tilted the lady's plastic bottle, popped a tablet into his mouth and then swallowed it down. He was completely satisfied with his own sagacity and the broad smile beaming from his face was accurately reflected in the bureau's mirror. A full minute passed without any change in Fred's joyful demeanor or any alteration in his physical excellence.

Then there was a slow subtle modification in the appearance of Barker's facial features. Wrinkles began to show, his flesh became flaccid and began sagging heavily under the man's eyes and chin, and soon age-marks developed on his arms and hands. Fred felt arthritis and rheumatism rampaging in his knees, elbows, shoulders and fingers. Thousands of grayish hairs sprouted from his scalp and the new undesirable white hairs soon easily enveloped and outnumbered their jet-black counterparts. The totally shocked fellow was aging at the rate of a year a second, and after a minute's duration, the pathetic man atrociously looked as if he were a hundred-year-old decrepit invalid.

Ten seconds later the infirmed fellow's flimsy anatomy collapsed upon the plush red and blue carpet. Three seconds later Fred Barker's heart stopped beating and then his lungs ceased breathing. The man's body quickly disintegrated into a small dust mound inside his casual blue denim jeans and his white cotton shirt.

The *Eternal Youth Corporation* Multi-Vitamin and Mineral bottle had rolled from Fred Barker's right hand and came to rest upon the red and blue carpet, and the small print facing up ironically read, '*Important: For Women Only!*'

"Time Vigilantes"

Michael Daniels stood erect before the austere-looking judge and next to his state appointed defense attorney in the crowded *Camden County Courthouse*. A solemn but confused expression ornamented Daniels small facial features. The bailiff stood at attention left of the elevated seat on the judge's platform. The black robed New Jersey public official austerely stared down at the accused through thick bifocals resting on the bridge of his nose.

"Michael Daniels, raise your right hand and place your left palm over the *Holy Bible!"* instructed the bailiff. "Now, do you swear to tell the truth, the whole truth and nothing but the absolute truth so help you God!"

"Yes sir," came the almost inaudible reply.

"Michael Daniels, how do you plead?" Judge Matthew Dixon asked.

"I think not guilty," the shy young man answered in a low hoarse voice.

"Are you certain?" the seemingly inflexible courtroom judge adamantly asked. "Could you speak a little louder and repeat your plea for everyone present to hear. And please don't say the word *think*. It's a subjective word that suggests uncertainty. Now Mr. Daniels, you' should either plead guilty or not guilty!"

"I plead not guilty!" the defendant accused of first-degree murder firmly stated.

"Counselor, have you adequately advised the defendant of his *Constitutional Rights* and of the possibility of a lesser voluntary manslaughter plea bargain should he have instead pleaded 'guilty'?" the by the book judicial authority asked the tall lean defense attorney.

"Yes Your Honor," Attorney Mark Brookes replied. "The defendant is very obstinate in that particular matter, insisting that he was unaware of any malicious intent on *his* part upon committing the alleged act."

"But Counselor, must I remind you that twenty-one other highly suspicious deaths had occurred at the *Echelon Mall* on the evening of May 20, 2002! Twenty-two people, many of them children, teenagers and perfectly healthy adults suddenly collapsed and died for no apparent reason. If convicted," Judge Dixon continued, "Michael Daniels might also be implicated in the other twenty-one bizarre mysterious deaths."

"In all due respect Your Honor," Attorney Mark Brookes indicated, "my client claims to know nothing about the other twenty-one inexplicable deaths that had transpired at the *Echelon Mall* on the night of Monday, May 20, 2002. The county's *Medical Examiner* and the best forensics' professionals in New Jersey haven't a clue as to a satisfactory logical explanation for the exact cause of the other twenty-one deaths other than cessation of vital signs," the gaunt-looking defense lawyer nobly stated. "The cause is a baffling enigma to the state's most expert investigators. The exact cause is too difficult to discern for even the most sophisticated and knowledgeable experts to identify."

"Very well, Counselor," the dignified judge sanctimoniously replied as he then sat still as a statue in his elevated black leather chair. "Do you have anything else to disclose before I direct the witness to take the stand and ask the prosecutor to proceed with his opening statement?"

"Yes, for the record," Attorney Mark Brookes elaborated, "I would like to have it entered that the identity of the victim remains unknown. The deceased had no wallet, no credentials, no *Social Security* card, no driver's license and no credit cards in his possession. The only things *he* had in his pocket were ten and twenty dollar bills, four hundred and seventy dollars total cash. The fingerprints on the bills matched none on record anywhere. The victim was shopping alone at the time of his demise, and no one in the mall knew his name. And," the State Appointed Counsel proceeded, "my client believes that the murder victim had possibly been involved in the killing of the twenty-one other victims at the *Echelon Mall* and that the anonymous murder victim possibly had an accomplice in performing those nefarious criminal acts."

"Is *Exhibit A* the device believed to be the murder weapon?" the judge prudently asked the county prosecutor. "I'd like to examine it when the questioning commences."

"Yes Your Honor," the chief Camden County District Attorney responded. "If you'll notice," Jeffrey Jensen suggested holding the unique object up to the judge while wearing sheer plastic surgical gloves, "our chief investigators believe that this instrument is some ingenious multi-functional weapon, some sort of organic tissue disintegrator," the county prosecutor expounded. "When pointed at a person, we believe it activates a distinct invisible death ray that instantly makes heart, liver and kidneys stop functioning. Our forensics' experts experimented with this device at the *SPCA* and satisfactorily demonstrated its properties by killing three dogs and two cats that were about to be put to sleep."

A roar broke out from the huge audience seated in the crammed courthouse. Judge Matthew Dixon pounded his gavel on his elevated desk-podium yelling, "Order in this court! Order in this court! Any further gallery outbursts will result in immediate removal, and I hereby instruct the bailiff and the other court security officers on duty of my intent!"

After silence had been re-established Judge Dixon again addressed the accused. "Michael Daniels, before I accept your earnest plea, clarify one thing for me. Did *you* know that the object in the prosecutor's hands was a murder weapon at the time of the alleged murder incident?"

"No Your Honor, I didn't!" the defendant emphatically answered. "It looks rather peculiar, doesn't it, sort of like a microphone with a flashlight head at one end, with three strange switches in the middle. That's really all I know about the thing, other than it was only in my hands for about ten seconds."

"Very well then Mr. Daniels," Judge Matthew Dixon assented, "the court accepts your plea of *Not Guilty*. We shall now hear opening statements and relevant arguments for Case Number 2943, State of New Jersey, County of Camden versus Michael Anthony Daniels."

* * * * * * * * * * * *

In the year 2370, the *Democratic* and *Republican* parties had become extinct because their political persuasions no longer met the changing socio-economic needs of American society. The fledgling *Neo-Puritan Party* came into power in the United States in 2376 following a bloody and devastating thirteen-year civil war between the radical left-wing *Libertarians* and the conservative right-wing *New Age Moralists*. Within a year stringent elements were set into motion to prevent a repeat of or a continuation of the horrible national catastrophe that had been courageously fought between cities *(Libertarians)* and rural towns *(New Age Moralists)* all over the nation.

In 2377, *District Military SWAT* squads were authorized to dispatch "moral vigilantes" to patrol city streets, slums, ghettos and drug-infested middle-class urban neighborhoods. Those "behavioral reformers" were not only assigned to enforce the nation's new laws but also to monitor the accepted practice of America's customs, traditions and favorable social habits. When law and "social order" had been forcibly re-established throughout the land, "moral vigilantes" were then delegated in teams of two to time-travel to the past. Their assigned objective was to punish "ancestral violators" that did not conform to the "high moral standards" based on "common sense" that constituted the rigid principles of the newly implemented *Neo-Puritan* philosophy.

Zentar and Grel were veteran "moral vigilantes" who had been working together for seven years since the quelling of the last significant *Libertarian* upheaval. The two highly decorated time-warriors ambled to the designated "Year 2002 Locker Room" to change into light-dyed blue denim jeans, black tee-shirts and spring denim jackets to simulate the clothing worn by males of the era that they would soon be visiting.

"What's your assignment?" Zentar asked Grel. "Or is it the usual search and destroy mission? I'm glad we both have only ten more years until retirement."

Grel opened a sealed envelope that contained his "Vital Instructions." "It says," the Time Vigilante read aloud, "proceed to *Echelon Mall,* Voorhees, New Jersey, May 20, 2002 from seven to eight p.m. Grel, you are hereby delegated and elevated to the distinguished *Non-Smoking in Public Places Patrol.* Efficiently eliminate anyone you find smoking in public. Feel free Officer Grel to exercise your judgment when it comes down to life or death situations."

"That's only right," Zentar agreed with the new edict formulated by the *District Moral Code Commander.* "People should be more considerate of those that don't smoke. I mean," Zentar momentarily paused to organize his justification, "I mean Grel it's bad enough that people are so stupid destroying their own lungs and bodies with hungry cancer cells. But if the lunatics are so addicted to nicotine then they should be smart enough to only smoke cigars and cigarettes in the privacy of their own homes. People should have the decency to not inhale and exhale contaminated toxic fumes in public places and jeopardize the health of other human beings."

"You're right on the money," Grel concurred with his loyal partner in moral law and social values' enforcement. "If people are ignorant enough to abuse the health of others by expelling quantities of smoke into the air," the time vigilante haughtily hypothesized and opined, "then Zentar, those stupid people must face the severe consequences without the expense of court appearances, police reports and jail incarceration. We just zap them with our *Internal Organ Destabilizers*," Grel said as the time policeman examined his splendid weapon that looked somewhat like a black microphone with a flashlight head attached on the front end.

"Aren't you going to ask me what my special assignment is?" Zentar coaxed as he ripped open his "Confidential Orders" envelope. "You know Grel, we both spent an entire week studying the speech patterns and mannerisms of these year 2002 freaks and I feel no compunction about killing the defective units."

"Okay, you're my partner," Grel admitted to Zentar, "so naturally you're heading to a place called the *Echelon Mall* with me. But what specific detail must *you* home in on? Are you going to kill the passive smokers inhaling the nicotine and tar from the active puffers?"

"Ha, ha, ha," Zentar bellowed in a rare display of emotion. "I've been assigned to the *Elite No Kissing in Public Patrol*. Anyone caught showing affection in public is to be executed on the spot. Grel, everyone knows that showing affection in public breeds self-centered spoiled, bratty children and makes infatuated adults such repulsive ingrates that they're then instinctively governed by hormones and not by reason. Hey Grel," Zentar expounded, "tell me how many people you've killed this year while on *Vigilante Patrol?* Have you kept a record?"

"Why yes," Grel acknowledged and confirmed. "I've killed three hundred and fifty-six in the past twelve months while on 'Affection Stakeout' and a thousand seven hundred and fifty three total for all of my various *Vigilante Patrol* assignments."

"Wow! You're several hundred executions ahead of me!" Zentar exclaimed with admiration. "I'll have to accelerate my eradicator button on this particular expedition," the moral crusader seriously stated as he made a last minute adjustment to a side dial on his very lethal weapon. "I have some serious catching up to do. Ya' know Grel," Zentar concluded and stated, "I like these blue denim jeans I have on a lot better than our soft-plastic uniforms we have to wear. Maybe I'll stay a while, retire and live out my life as a freelance assassin in the year 2002!"

"Don't become too corrupted by the crime and moral decay of the year 2002," Grel sincerely warned, "or I might soon be assigned by the *District Commander* to exterminate you! Make sure you have the five-hundred dollars in 2002 cash to buy food and merchandise with!"

Zentar and Grel believed in the importance and the necessity of their assigned "morality enforcement patrols." In their briefing from Captain Dorn, they had learned that Year 2002 Americans were reprehensibly egotistical, so despicable, so unappreciative and also so completely and intolerably aberrant of the fundamentals of social organization. Moral Patrols were often officially commissioned to journey to the past and assassinate individuals caught smoking, kissing, loitering in public places, cursing or spitting on public sidewalks or acting uncouth, boisterous and obnoxious inside public areas and squares. The Time Vigilantes' actions were justified from their point of view because both men had been wholly indoctrinated into a strict moral discipline code that made each hunter think unilaterally in identical idea-interpretation-reaction patterns. Both Grel and Zentar behaved and obeyed like similar well' synchronized murder machines.

"I particularly enjoy exterminating fat people," Grel proudly boasted. "There's no satisfactory reason or explanation for anyone weighing three hundred pounds and walking around a shopping mall eating a triple-scooped chocolate ice cream sugar-cone. When I see a person like that I deviate from my prescribed orders and zap that lousy violator right on the spot."

"Now you're talking my language," Zentar related and agreed. "*Neo-Puritans* have the right idea and I'm glad they emerged victorious from the war and totally vanquished the major opposition parties. Fat people, invalids, ugly people and cripples all carry bad genes," the cyber-policeman confidently maintained. "Eliminate them as the *Internal Security Council* has intelligently mandated and big expensive *future* drains on our fine government

78

and on our now strong economy have been swiftly excised out. Cancel out problems in the past to ensure a moral and prosperous future, that's my philosophy along with the *Internal Security Council's* positive thinking too."

"Just remember," Grel reminded his hell-bent-for-leather comrade, "you've been delegated by the government to kill violators kissing in public. Zentar, as a general rule you're not allowed to terminate corpulent, lame, ugly or feeble wheel-chaired senior citizens at random on this specific scouting foray into enemy territory. You're to only kill those kinds of idiots if you don't come across a lot of inconsiderate public kissers. And above all else," Grel joked while showing little conscience, "don't kill any smokers. That's *my* personal responsibility."

America in the year 2380 AD was a tranquil civilization devoid of the ravages of "frustrating social diseases." The ultra-right-wing *Neo-Puritans* had transformed men, women and children into "Reverse Transcendentalists," or a society that valued thinking over feeling. The edicts and mandates coming out of Washington had maintained "Man is a rational, intellectual creature capable of learning, discovering, analyzing, studying and inventing." Expression' of emotions while in public areas was regarded by the government as an extension of "overt animal monkey behavior."

Expressions of feelings and emotions were not only at first discouraged but after the "moral revolution" were' later suppressed. *Neo-Puritan* government officials both despised and deplored demonstrations of affection in public. And when violators were caught on tape by spy cameras located at every city intersection and at every town traffic light across the continental United States, then the "criminals" were apprehended by "Storm Police" and then put into stocks and placed on public display in the center of town or in a city square to be publicly scorned and ridiculed. The "immoral criminals" were then mocked, spit upon, slapped and humiliated by amused bystanders and by righteous passing citizens.

Zentar and Grel were both aware that all aspects of life had to be logical and rational, including law, morality, behavior and even death. Everything had a scientific explanation and was transmitted as "basic educational truth" to the public via schools and via the government-controlled mass media. The entire society was functioning in a precise manner like a well-oiled machine.

According to the *Neo-Puritan Party* leadership, the elimination of "animalistic emotional behavior" would make the achievement of "rational reality" more readily attainable. Scientific principles such as "cause and effect" were taught as factors that govern human behavior as well as technology also, so if a "criminal" committed a public fault, then his or her action was judged to be the "cause" of a predictable "effect" (punishment and public ridicule). The new social science code of law was molded to be an exact science similar to chemistry and physics, and psychology, religion and sociology were banned subjects in all of the nation's colleges and universities. Such were the narrow-minded but extremely effective teachings and practices of the stern-faced *Neo-Puritans*.

"Are you ready to enforce social justice upon idiotic fools and insane hypocrites in the year 2002?" Grel asked his highly motivated companion.

"Our beam transmitters are pre-programmed to the Men's Room just outside the 'Food Court at the *Echelon Mall*, Voorhees, New Jersey. Check your gauge coordinates," Zentar commanded his vigilante colleague. "It's almost time to initiate our essential mission to eradicate future decadence!"

"Everything is desirable!" Grel alerted. "Let's synchronize our time-space alteration beams."

"All right, contact and away we go!" Zentar directed. "Let's have a blast into the past!"

* * * * * * * * * * * *

Three men were washing their hands in sinks and a boy was combing his hair as Zentar and Grel suddenly crystallized behind them in the men's lavatory mirror's reflection. The two futuristic space-time visitors immediately turned right and stepped out of the *Echelon Mall's* tidy Men's Room in a well' disciplined military cadence as if nothing extraordinary had ever happened.

The four bewildered individuals looked at one another with astonished expressions on their faces, all sharing the same "mass hallucination" and "group illusion," shrugging their shoulders in disbelief at what their eyes had just perceived but what their minds desired not to recognize.

Inside the "Food Court Pavilion" Zentar and Grel decided it was time to split up, promising to rendezvous again at 8 p.m. in the same tidy Men's Room for the return passage to Precinct Headquarters, 837 Arch Street, Philadelphia, Pennsylvania, year 2380.

"See you in an hour," Zentar predicted to his very efficient comrade. "Don't get lost in any lingerie departments!" the Time Vigilante facetiously added.

"Make sure you don't expire any smokers," Grel reminded his determined patriotic colleague. "And don't be a maverick. Only focus on and zap kissers with your *Internal Organ Destabilizer* and leave the nasty despicable smokers to me."

"You do have a propensity for manufacturing your own brand of propaganda," Zentar volleyed back. "You'd make a damned good politician now that lawyers have been made illegal!"

Grel meandered to his left at the *Echelon Mall* Food Court's crowded custard and ice cream concession and Zentar remained stationary inside the colorful "Food Court Pavilion" searching for potential recipients of his formidable death ray. 'This isn't exactly random killing,' the well-trained assassin thought. 'Random means to kill anybody violating the country's future moral codes, but I'm especially in quest of people showing excessive affection in public at the wrong time and at the wrong place,' Zentar rationalized and considered. 'I'm not governed by any narrow time schedule or by any specified itinerary to perform my vital service. I only have an agenda that will make future generations more cerebral and less animalistic and emotional. Raw emotions are merely extensions of the basic animal state of existence.'

Zentar alertly observed a young couple embracing in a long customer line in front of the *Food Court's* pizza concession. 'They must be low-mentality teenagers infatuated with one another's *animal magnetism*,' Zentar speculated and concluded. 'Married couples usually are tired of each other after a month of sex and don't care to show public affection like these unfortunate adolescent imbeciles are about to.'

Predictably, the acne-faced high school students' mouths came close together, and in another three seconds, their lips met. Soon the young lovers were engaged in an extended kiss. The futuristic commando was very adroit at his chosen trade and without even raising his deadly weapon to his eyes, he easily extinguished the two young students of *Cupid* with two instantaneous waist-high invisible laser jets pulsating from his remarkable weapon.

No one milling around the *Food Court Pavilion* noticed Zentar's efficient evil executions, which had indeed been performed very stealthily and very deftly. Two youthful bodies collapsed to the tan-tiled mall floor and then a chorus of hysterical screams permeated throughout that corner sector of *the Food Court Pavilion.*

The successful time traveler assassin casually sauntered in the direction of the custard and ice cream station situated in the middle of the *Echelon Mall* Food Court adjacent to the colossal double-decked indoor shopping center's main traffic corridor. 'Grel and I will be out of here is less than an hour once we meet our quotas,' the confident killer reckoned, 'and the incompetent police won't be able to coordinate mall camera pictures from all of the selective assassinations for over two hours. Even if the moronic cops cordon off all entrances and exits to the mall,' Zentar slyly concluded, 'we'll both easily escape *their* wimpy dragnet by simply disappearing into *time* while shrewdly eluding being trapped in *space.*'

In front of the *Pretzel and Donut Factory*, Zentar spotted a male and a female passionately kissing. It didn't matter if they were husband and wife or simply an engaged couple about to be married. Public affection was a taboo that had to be purged from the Year 2002 to guarantee society's future health in the Year 2380. Zentar wasted little time reacting to the capricious display rather promptly and effectively.

'Silly frivolous fools!' Zentar evaluated. 'They ought to know better and have more consideration for the public that has to be unnecessarily exposed to *their* juvenile antics. *They* should know that in the future, television shows', movies and soap operas aren't allowed to have kissing scenes in them. Dumb subhuman cretins!' Zentar imagined. 'In the future, people simply *like* each other and are compelled by law to *like* everyone in their society. *Love* is too strong of a word to use in 2380 AD. *Love* is just an ideal, a distant longing for a girl or for a woman, like *Don Quixote* had felt in literature for *Dulcinea,'* Zentar mentally assessed. 'That's what *love* should really be in the Year 2002, but the word *like* is exactly how the abstraction *love* is described in 2380, and *like* never involves affection!'

As Zentar reached into his jacket to wrap his fingers around his trusty "violators' zapper," the futuristic visitor wondered what it would be like to actually kiss a woman. Realizing the folly of his rampant imagination, the dedicated space-time patrolman squeezed the side of his awesome weapon, and in five brief seconds a pair of invisible death rays had "destroyed" the "two human examples" lying motionless on the tile floor.

The very dangerous time commando scanned the area above the store facades for mall surveillance cameras. After completing *his* cursory camera inspection thirty feet away from the fallen affection victims, Zentar strolled to another section of the mall, pretending to be one of many apathetic eyewitnesses that wanted nothing to do with the travails and fates of the already dead mall patrons. Shouts and gasps were heard as alarmed and appalled shoppers rushed to the scene to view the macabre charred spectacles lying on the elaborate brown-tiled floor designs.

Three hundred feet down the busy mall corridor Zentar encountered two gay women holding hands. Lesbian behavior was regarded as "an abomination" by the rigid-morals' *Neo-Puritan Party,* which staunchly condemned all forms of homosexual activity. 'They don't even have to kiss each other for me to be motivated to kill them,' the time visitor wickedly thought. 'This human vermin disgusts me and turns my stomach sour. I can even taste the foul putrid digestive juice pumping its way up to my mouth! I hate scummy queers even more than I despise public affection!' the futuristic soldier's twisted mind banefully decided. 'I can't wait to zap these scurrilous licentious violators!'

In another ten seconds, two female corpses lay prone on the brown-tile floor amidst yells, hollers and shouts from exasperated mall shoppers that happened to be in the vicinity. Zentar chuckled to himself' as he slyly feigned looking inside a glass partition of an exclusive men's store, coyly studying several pair of fancy dress shoes. 'Don't need those suckers!' he thought with a big smirk on his face. 'I'll take combat boots any day,' the Time Vigilante grinned as his eyes glanced down at the brown penny loafers on *his* feet.

Two distraught security guards followed by three anxious Voorhees Township policemen sprinted by the shoe display in the opposite direction racing toward the crime scene. Zentar nonchalantly shuffled his way toward the expansive entrance to a prominent department store. 'Those ugly female faggots got what they deserved,' he mentally reviewed with great satisfaction. 'If they want to be lesbians, then the damned perverts should be lesbians outside of public scrutiny in the privacy of their own homes. In the year 2380,' Zentar mused, 'even popular songs don't mention the words' kiss, affection or love, and I'm exclusively thinking about heterosexual relationships. Those female freaks are on their way to *Hell* right now, and that's exactly where the lecherous sinners belong! The *Devil* already owned their souls before I punctually eliminated them from this Earth!'

Zentar then stepped inside the enormous well' stocked department store and advanced through the perfume, jewelry and panty hose departments. In front of the dual ascending and descending escalators the callous human automaton witnessed a young kindergarten age' girl dashing up to an elderly woman yelling "Grandma', Grandma!" The affectionate young girl gave her grandmother a massive kiss on her lips and the elderly woman wholeheartedly reciprocated.

'There's no depth to their simple childish minds,' the enraged observer concluded. 'All' the two dolts know how to do is express shallow ideas of a need for security to each other!' Zentar angrily imagined with his eyes blazing red. 'They'll be executed on the basis of lacking mental depth and of showing a lack of regard for others in this public environment.'

The unbridled exhibition of genuine natural affection caused animosity to well' up inside Zentar's consciousness and ten seconds later, two still bodies lay dead on the department store floor amidst resounding screams from horrified mall customers and completely stunned sales personnel.

Zentar next entered and then took the elevator up to the second floor and exited into the gigantic store's sporting goods department. Immediately, the Time Vigilante's perceptive eyes detected and focused on a mother loudly smooching her baby's face and the overt sound of exaggerated affection and loud cooing only intensified the time assassin's rage. 'Stupid frivolous asinine behavior!' the commando's mind criticized. 'That foolish woman doesn't realize that true happiness comes from achieving, from producing, from inventing, from thinking and from exploring the limits of human intelligence. That kid will never be able to have the patience and discipline to write a book or to accomplish anything great in life that requires a lot of thought,' Zentar mentally criticized and analyzed. 'That mother doesn't realize that true happiness results from satisfaction being derived from

84

success. A kid who is too secure is afraid to fail, and failure is necessary to build character and integrity,' Zentar convinced himself as his mind reiterated certain moral axioms that military instructors had incessantly inculcated into *his* very complex thought patterns. 'What ever happened to parent-centered families? Child-centered families breed demanding doltish offspring that are lazy, contented, egocentric and that are falsely praised for just existing and that are undeservingly doted on for not achieving anything special in life or for that matter, ever achieving anything mediocre!'

Before the highly trained Time Vigilante administered his fatal death ray, some other negative thoughts swam through his very upset mind. 'Lazy spoiled brats are the result of this silly ridiculous affectionate behavior mental sickness! Instead of children imitating mature parents, parents in this derelict socially chaotic age of 2002 are absurdly imitating immature children and acting like two-year-olds themselves'! Whatever happened to the notion that children should be seen and not heard or touched?'

A minute later the mother and her infant lay dead in front of the sporting goods department's pyramid baseball bat display. After a sales clerk desperately yelled for assistance, a crowd of delirious and hysterical curiosity seekers gathered around the helpless victims, who both would soon be riding in local coroner's hearses rather than in hospital ambulances.

The very proficient time murderer paced to the front of the department store where seven beleaguered police officers rushed by *his* slow methodical gait. 'Life in my future time might be cold, calculating and analytical,' Zentar reckoned, 'but it's certainly more objective and rational than in 2002. Little is subjective and emotional in 2380, and I *like* it that way. Everything makes sense. It bothers me when adults act like children when parents and grandparents should be setting models of mature behavior for youngsters to imitate,' Zentar reasoned and justified. 'The people of this age are so primitive and so un-evolved. The parents slobber all over and delight in licking their babies' faces much the same as primitive apes do with their young. It looks so sloppy and it sounds so awful when they suck on each other as if the mother and kid were lollipops. It sounds and looks like mother monkeys licking and sucking their helpless chimpanzee offspring. That's exactly what it looks like and what it sounds like,' the Time Vigilante thought as turmoil and confusion abounded around him. 'These damned mentally underdeveloped humans of 2002 haven't yet evolved beyond the gorilla level of existence! Human intelligence must ultimately triumph over animalistic feelings!'

Zentar's cruel heart lusted for more homicides, so the human killing machine entered the mall's *McDonald's* and sat down at a booth without ordering anything. According to schedule in fifteen minutes he would be meeting Grel, who had been creating *his* own premeditated havoc with unwary smokers all over the panic-stricken mall.

Glancing to his right, the conscience-less time slayer from the future observed two small children across the aisle. The moral vigilante surreptitiously suspected the two were brother and sister as they were innocently and voluntarily kissing one another. As usual, the toddlers' parents were preoccupied chatting and they and their pristine children were oblivious to the killing machine's cunning scrutiny.

'What's wrong with people of this peculiar era?' Zentar wondered. 'They all seem to want to be targets of my wrath and they all appear to have death' wishes. Don't they know that they're exchanging millions and millions of germs and spreading infection with their slimy tongues and wet mouths licking each other?' the crazed highly-disciplined homicide enforcer remembered from one of his military indoctrination lectures.

Then the moral vigilante's temper escalated to an even higher level. 'Affection merely breeds complacency and a false sense of security,' he thought and truly believed. 'It never leads to suspicion and the enactment of intelligent survival behavior. That's why lions rule the grasslands and antelopes don't. The lion is more intelligent than the antelope. The lion is the hunter and the antelope the prey. Don't these stupid people understand that only intelligent and wary creatures survive in a world fraught with competition and struggle! Too much security will lead to societal decay and to cultural decline!' Zentar vengefully thought. 'These disturbing entitlement-oriented kids will never enjoy the much more meaningful abstractions in life such as honor, happiness from achievement, justice, courage, courtesy, beauty and truth. All these spoiled conditioned brats know is security resulting from affection, and too much security is evil and will eventually lead to *Western Civilization's* decline!' thought the brainwashed moral vigilante to his very receptive will and *Neo-Puritan* value system.

Zentar instinctively reached into his denim jacket's pocket and removed the power source for his deadly death ray *Internal Organ and Tissue Disintegrator*. His first impulse was to warily gaze to his left to ascertain that his villainous act would not be observable to any normally inattentive *McDonald's* diners.

Much to *his* astonishment Zentar's eyes recognized Darf, a member of the *Libertarian Party's* Stealth Secret Police, aiming *his* death ray gun directly at the enemy he had readily identified and had been astutely stalking inside the *Echelon Mall*.

The thought of 'Survival' dominated Zentar's machine-like precision mind and as he quickly ducked down under the booth's table, Darf's ray blast flashed across and above the intended victim's head. Ironically Darf had performed Zentar's duty by inadvertently and unintentionally killing the little boy and his sister affectionately kissing one another in the adjacent *McDonald's* booth.

Seeing an opportunity for escape, Zentar slid out of his smooth green leather booth, crawled a distance of ten feet on the floor, rose to his knees and then hustled as fast as his legs could carry him out of the fast food establishment and in his haste to safety, accidentally leaving his extraordinary zap disintegrator behind during all of the mass confusion.

Michael Daniels, a mentally challenged but dependable *McDonald's Restaurant* employee, recognized that Zentar had left his personal property on the light green leather seat. Daniels ceased wiping down the top of a neighboring table, ignored the delirious exclamations of shock and fright around him, picked up the strange alien weapon and instinctively pursued its owner into the main mall shopping area.

"Sir, Sir, you left this inside the store!' Michael Daniels shouted at the top of his lungs. "Please stop and let me give it to you!"

A young child broke away from his mother's grasp and wobbled directly into Michael Daniel's path. The mentally challenged high school special needs student leaped into the air to hurtle over the toddler, and when the teenager's right wrist made contact with the brown rectangular tiled floor, the weapon was activated. An invisible deadly ray was discharged and immediately paralyzed the fleeing Zentar, who immediately dropped to the floor and was dead in ten seconds.

* * * * * * * * * * * *

Judge Matthew Dixon carefully studied Michael Daniel's pallid face and asked Camden County Prosecutor Jeffrey Jensen to remove *his* surgical gloves and hand them to him so that the court official could closely examine the "alleged murder weapon."

"May I remind the judge that the defendant Michael Daniels is a mentally challenged high school student working part time at *McDonald's* on a special state-sponsored school work program," Defense Attorney Mark Brookes glibly interrupted.

Judge Matthew Dixon carefully examined the alien lethal ray expeller. His thumb accidentally slid against an inconspicuous side-control as coincidentally the "flashlight head" had been pointing straight into the judge's face. A secondary ray was emitted and Judge Dixon instantaneously vanished from sight.

The flabbergasted bailiff and the amazed police guards on courtroom duty rushed forward with drawn revolvers. The shocked courtroom audience was unaware that Judge Matthew Dixon had accidentally teleported himself to the year 2380 where his "good workable mind" would be thoroughly infiltrated and indoctrinated to become a member-in-training of the "Honorable Neo-Puritan Moral Vigilante Police Patrol."

"The Hotel Delaware"

Superstitious people believe and attest that strange incidents often occur on February 29 of every *Leap Year*. I had never placed too much credence in that unscientific claim until Tuesday, February 29, 2004, which unfortunately is a date I will certainly remember forever. Let me fully explain my accursed dilemma so that all will comprehend the true nature of my misery. The courtesy of another's sympathy and understanding will be greatly appreciated. I realize that my tale will seem both illogical and incredible to anyone interpreting it, yet I believe I must share its veracity.

A *Leap Year* has three hundred and sixty-six days on the annual calendar', one more twenty-four hour interval than that which exists in a normal year. Greenwich, England scientists and concerned astronomers have adjusted the mechanics of the moon and months to interface with the earth's revolution around the sun because a quarter of a day is lost each normal year when coordinating those particular solar system relationships. To accurately adjust for the quarter-day time discrepancy in the earth's elliptical orbit around the sun, February 29 was created on the post medieval *Gregorian Calendar* (developed in the 1580s by Pope Gregory), which we still honor today after the old Julian Calendar (developed in 46 B.C. under the reign of Julius Caesar) had been discarded.

Some *Leap Years* are unluckier than others. Every year divisible by the number four (lets' say the year 2004 or 2008) is generally regarded in common knowledge as a legitimate bona fide *Leap Year*. No problem! So far so good! But every year divisible by a hundred is *not* a *Leap Year* unless that particular year is also divisible by four hundred; then it is still defined as a legitimate, bona fide *Leap Year*. For example, the years 1800, 1900, 2100 and 2200 AD are *not Leap Years* because they can't be divided by four hundred. Conversely, the Year 2000 *was* recognized as a legitimate, bona fide *Leap Year* because it *was* divisible by four hundred.

A person born on this planet Earth has a one in 1,506 chance of being born on February 29 of a *Leap Year,* but nevertheless 4.1

million individuals living around the globe have made their official grand appearance on that weird day and of that large number, 188,000 of them live in the United States. Before February 29, 2004, I had always felt sorry for people born on February 29 because their birthdays arrive only once every four years. Now I feel sorry for myself' for not staying at home on that ill-starred date. Allow me to fully explain my dilemma.

Some humans on this planet have attempted to conceal the bad omens that are associated with *Leap Year*. For example *Sadie Hawkins Day* is celebrated on February 29 when single women once every four years are permitted to abandon traditional courting practice and chase after or propose marriage to men, thus attempting to make the "unlucky aspects" of that ominous day appear less threatening and more tolerable to the human race. But I can earnestly assert from my own personal experience that February 29, 2004 is a day I feel compelled to remember for all eternity. Soon you'll learn why.

I had made an appointment for Tuesday, February 29, 2004 to meet the book editor of a small publishing company at eleven a.m. at the *Regal Restaurant*, Baltimore Avenue, at the southern end of Ocean City, Maryland. I had been an arcade owner and operator of *Dealers Choice Games* at 410 South Boardwalk, Ocean City, Maryland, from 1967-'81. So naturally I was quite familiar with the city and with the reputable *Regal Restaurant*, which was one of my favorite breakfast and lunch haunts when I had been an industrious summer boardwalk businessman in that resort city. I was really looking forward to making the business/pleasure trip down to the Maryland shore.

The editor's publishing firm was located in Annapolis, Maryland, and so Ocean City was a convenient halfway destination for us to rendezvous to discuss my book submission that had attracted David Evans attention. A contract had been signed by me and mailed to the publishing company. All I had to do was drive seventy miles from my Hammonton, New Jersey home' to Cape May, catch the 7:30 a.m. ferry across *Delaware Bay* to Lewes, Delaware and then drive another hour down the Atlantic Coast to Ocean City, Maryland. My only regret was that the very busy editor had scheduled our "brunch engagement" at 11 a.m. on the very inauspicious date, February 29, 2004.

My wife wanted to borrow my merlot-colored *Nissan Maxima* to impress some of her friends with *our* new driving machine, so

90

I had to settle driving her light brown *Nissan Altima* from Hammonton seventy miles south down to Cape May, New Jersey. I left my home at six a.m., figuring I had more than sufficient time to make my easy connection with the *Cape May-Lewes Ferry* since I had conducted similar trips hundred of times before.

Driving down Bellevue Avenue in Hammonton, I accidentally ran over a board lying in the street that had nails protruding face-up. I felt the *Altima's* steering wheel wobble when I drove another three miles to the *Atlantic City Expressway* entrance. Five miles in the direction of Atlantic City I frantically veered my wife's brown automobile into the *Frank Farley Rest Area* and quickly inflated the hissing tire with air.

Speeding down the *Expressway* at eighty-miles an hour, I thought I had had a hallucination of sorts. I had an uncanny sensation that I had skidded off the right shoulder of the highly traveled highway and that the light brown *Nissan Altima* had entered a pine barrens' forest and had then slammed into a tree, knocking me unconscious. 'I really didn't get a good night's sleep!' I remember thinking after surviving the rather surreal manifestation that seemingly featured a very real impact. 'I must get to the ferry before this confounded front tire goes flat. Then I will have really *missed the boat*!' my mind mused. 'I mustn't disappoint the editor by having a real collision. That accident was merely a wild figment of my imagination!'

In my wandering mind the same "air injection" of the affected tire was duplicated fifteen miles down the *Expressway* when I exited the toll thoroughfare at Pleasantville and then I again anxiously repeated the nerve-racking inflation procedure. After taking the *Expressway* to the *Garden State Parkway* I had to again stop at a *Parkway Service Area* and fill the tire with air and then desperately continue my extremely harrowing journey south. At Cape May I anxiously drove into a gas station and repeated the left front tire inflation a fourth time until I finally and gratefully made it to the ferry dock at 7:20. My mind was in a very paranoid state from all of the duress that had converted a supposedly pleasant ride into a living nightmare.

When I pulled-up to the *Cape May-Lewes Ferry* tollbooth I turned up the volume on the *Altima's* stereo radio and then paid the unwary grim-faced female collector the exact amount for crossing the bay. She never heard the air hissing and sizzling out of my left front tire. I was too arrogant and proud to understand that the tire traumas were seemingly attempting to warn me not to cross the *Delaware Bay.*

I drove the light brown *Altima* forward and boarded the ferry and at the time I felt haughty and confident that I had cleverly outsmarted a major obstacle (by fooling the apathetic toll collector) caused by unlucky February 29, 2004. The ferry's entrance ramp was raised, the ship's loud horns sounded, and next I perceived that the huge one-hundred-twenty-vehicle capacity boat had gently slid out of its mooring.

I smugly sat in my wife's car, speculating that I would exit it a half-hour later and report my flat tire predicament to the captain when the ferry was halfway across *Delaware Bay.* 'The captain will get several of his crew-members to go down with a can of air-sealant and inflate my front tire so that I can safely make it down to Ocean City without further incident,' I cleverly imagined. 'I've outsmarted the ferry personnel by making my tire problem *their* tire problem to solve! I can always buy a brand new front tire at a service station in Ocean City.'

A half-hour finally elapsed on my watch. I casually got out of the *Altima*, inspected the front tire and immediately ascertained that it had indeed gone flat. 'Tires are only flat on the bottom!' I recollect humoring myself' with a popular joke.

My eyes glanced around and extraordinarily observed that the light brown *Altima* was the only car on the ferry, which (as I have mentioned) could easily carry and transport over a hundred similar-sized vehicles across the bay. Furthermore, after ascending the white metal steps to the top-deck, I detected that the ferry was enveloped in a very dense fog. I could barely see the familiar partially sunken concrete ship situated in the distance off of Cape May Point, but the famous *Cape May Lighthouse* was completely shrouded by the heavy veil of dense atmospheric haze that had descended on *Delaware Bay.*

Looking ahead south in the direction of the Delaware shoreline, I couldn't see any signs of land or of manmade structures. 'The fog's as thick as soup!' I evaluated. 'It's a good thing this ship has an adequate radar system!' I thankfully considered in an effort to allay my heightened anxiety.

Upon entering the main concession area I immediately recognized that something was very abnormal. 'Where are all the other passengers? I'm the only one in the entire room! Where are the waitresses and the food attendants? Nobody's on this cursed ship except me!' I quickly realized.

I wildly clambered up metal stairs to the captain's deck and attempted to open the door to his control room but the doorknob would not turn and the windowless white metal object would not budge. 'This is stranger than peculiar!' I nervously thought. 'This popular ferry has transformed into a mysterious ghost ship of some kind! Damned February 29!' I neurotically blamed that date. "Damned February 29, 2004!" I lustily screamed out into the apathetic dense *Delaware Bay* fog.

I investigated the entire ship and found no evidence of any other human being aboard. I anxiously searched in the Men's Room, in the lounge area, in the engine rooms, and even had the audacity to enter the forbidden "Ladies Room" but much to my disappointment and dismay, apparently I was the only person making the 'supernatural passage.' I recall wishing 'Please Lord, if only I could locate just one petrified passenger to provide me some semblance of comfort from my overwhelming apprehension. Then I'll feel a whole lot better,' I solemnly prayed.

My feet stepped to the ship's bow and I futilely held my left-hand up to my sweaty forehead, endeavoring to get a glimpse of some remote familiar landmark or perhaps hear a *Delaware Bay* oil tanker's horns. 'I've taken this ferry ride at least seven hundred times between 1967 and '81 transporting merchandise from family boardwalk stores in Ocean City, Maryland, Rehoboth Beach, Delaware and Atlantic City, New Jersey,' I remember thinking and analyzing. 'But this misadventure has got to be the most frightening seventeen mile crossing above and beyond any nightmare or seasickness I could ever have experienced!' I thought as my body trembled and my knees knocked together. 'There just has to be some feasible explanation!'

The ferry's eerie foghorn blasted three times and as I stared off into the distance, my eyes finally were able to identify a nebulous-looking familiar object, the first of two parallel jetties that had been constructed about a mile into the *Delaware Bay* on the Lewes, Delaware side. 'At last, something I know and recognize in this crazy horrifying mental jigsaw puzzle! Now I have some hope! Those jetties had been built to prevent beach erosion,' I recall concluding.

The captain-less ship then strangely deviated from its normal course (that I had memorized in my head) and slowly cutting through the very palpable fog, it turned left and then entered the channel between the two jetties instead of continuing straight ahead past them to the Lewes, Delaware dock. The vessel was now nearer to Cape Henlopen than to its appointed destination, the Lewes, Delaware terminal.

I felt an intense chill circulating throughout my stunned body. The combination of an overall sinister atmosphere and an accompanying damp mist was comparable in my mind to imagining me traveling to a close friend's funeral aboard a mysterious lost ghost ship adrift at sea. At least that was the odd-type of sensation or perception that my consciousness had been rationalizing.

The ferry sounded its loud foghorn one final time and then effortlessly glided and slowly eased into a berth (that was unfamiliar to me) on the Delaware shore. I was quite perturbed and distraught with my heart filled with distinct trepidation, not knowing whether my crazy misadventure was an actual experience or a fantastic arcane delusion. Overhead gears threaded with thick chains suddenly began rotating and next the exit ramp for cars and passengers squeakily descended. 'We've landed near Cape Henlopen and not near Lewes, the ferry's destination,' I recollect thinking. 'This is definitely not where *we're* supposed to be! Something's certainly amiss here!'

My pupils steadfastly gazed through the persistent dense fog and saw a vague illumination directly ahead. A dim light shone from a hand-held lantern and a shadowy figure was silhouetted behind the weak glow. As if my body and spirit had suddenly been magnetized, my legs reflexively began walking in the direction of the obscure figure holding the morbid lantern.

My mind was still aware of the light brown *Nissan Altima* parked near the ferry's bow but my heart and body could not resist the inexplicable potent force that was deliberately pulling and dragging me like an invisible tractor-beam to the ominous figure holding the ancient-looking lantern.

"Welcome to the *Hotel Delaware!*" the old white-bearded man ominously greeted. "Do not be afraid. I'm your host and your guide who will supervise your tenure here. I suppose you have many questions to ask me as most guests do."

94

"Who are you?" I tentatively inquired. "Why am I here? What's going on?"

"I am Diogenes," the ghostly character revealed, "and *you* are here dear visitor obviously because you're dead and your prodigious spirit desperately requires rest, rehabilitation and requiem. Come with me inside your new lodging," the grayish apparition dressed in ancient Greek garb communicated.

"And if I refuse?" I defiantly challenged. "What will be the consequences? What will be my punishment?"

"You have no say in the matter whatsoever," Diogenes grimly uttered. "You had surrendered your free will when your spirit escaped its confinement from inside your body. You have no choice as a dead entity other than to cooperate with my mandates. I can force you to perform any act that I want you to execute so don't resist my commands!" my pallid-faced ghostly guide explained. "Insolence will not be tolerated. You surrendered your free will when your spirit evacuated your body! Do you comprehend that basic truth?"

My emotions were dominated by shock and awe. I remember thinking, '*You've* spent thirty-five years of your life teaching public school kids English grammar, vocabulary, writing and literature, have finally reached retirement age, have begun a promising writing career and have sabotaged it all by suddenly becoming deceased on February 29th!'

My body reluctantly followed Diogenes away from the spooky ferry mooring and then we meandered through the thick fog in the direction of a dilapidated structure situated directly ahead. My restless spirit (or that element of it which still remained in my consciousness) demanded some plausible explanations from the hoary-looking man dressed in a wretched-looking ancient mendicant's dull gray robe.

"I must have died in the automobile accident on the *Expressway!*" I gasped in horror. "Diogenes, did I die in an automobile accident? I just have to know that to alleviate my nervousness!"

"What is an automobile?" the twenty-four-century old man asked. "It really doesn't matter what that is," he continued speaking like a verbal cadaver. "You're dead as a doormat and now charged in my professional custody, automobile or no automobile. Do you comprehend my words? The ideas and objects of your former world, of *my* former world, no longer interest me. They're both irrelevant and obsolete here!"

We slowly paced forward in the direction of the ominous-looking *Hotel Delaware*, which was now visibly outlined in the very thick mist with a rickety-looking shingle hanging on one hinge indicating my whereabouts. I found my guide's answer very incomprehensible (let alone reprehensible) but nevertheless quite intriguing. "Diogenes," I boldly said, "are you' the ancient Greek known to history as the *Cynic?*"

"You're quite a knowledgeable fellow because not too many souls make that association," my spooky host articulated, "and yes Stranger, you are correct in making that connection. You must read books to be aware of that academic fact!"

"But how have you gotten from ancient civilization to the United States in the year 2004, and where did you learn to speak perfect English?" I stammered.

"Please Sir, one question at a time," my new guardian insisted with a stern grimace featured on his ghostly and macabre-looking pale face. "I really don't know or care how I've arrived at *your* distant country. I can only tell you that once every three hundred and eighty-four years I'm moved and re-stationed by the unpredictable *Powers That Be* to a new drab and monotonous assignment in a new land. And finally," Diogenes proceeded with his fascinating monologue, "I've learned and conquered your language from conversing with other guests that have stayed or are staying at the *Hotel Delaware*. Does that answer satisfy your rather simplistic curiosity?"

"Well, somewhat!" I marveled and replied. "I had read about you in a college philosophy class," I nervously stated, "and you were notorious for diligently walking the streets with a lantern looking for the face of an honest man. Is that legend actually true? Is that why you're still carrying your lantern?"

"You're most perceptive and appear to be highly educated," my alert guide observed and reluctantly complimented. "Yes it is true, but historical truths are meaningless now, both to you and to me. The only significant truth that really matters is that we're both dead and that *you* must reside by Heaven's decree at the very serene *Hotel Delaware*. That is why the ferryboat delivered you to these obscure premises in that intense fog. Every time the mist settles I know I'll be hearing the ship's horns," the old withered specter lethargically related, "and then that blast is my

96

signal to come out from the hotel and cordially escort our latest guest inside. After that task is done my next responsibility is to make my most recent ward as comfortable as possible."

As my famous deceased guide and I paced up thirteen flimsy steps and gradually arrived at the *Hotel Delaware's* main entrance, the creaky door with un-oiled hinges slowly opened and Diogenes led me inside the musty building, which immediately reminded me of a dingy and despicable murky funeral home. Cobwebs, broken windows, bleak-looking dirty chandeliers and layers of dust everywhere suggested that the hotel for death-transients was a ruinous unkempt *deathtrap*.

"Diogenes, is it true what I've read in encyclopedias that you believed that wealth and honor are of little value because they do not help men lead just and moral lives?" I instinctively asked my laconic host. "I recollect that principle as being the cornerstone to your philosophy."

"All of those seemingly important old ideas are quite immaterial and irrelevant now," Diogenes glumly answered. "Virtue, honor, wealth and morality are no longer essential elements of behavior. If I were you," Diogenes imperatively cautioned, "I would ask fewer questions and then pay attention and learn the fundamental elements of my new environment. Just remember Sir', you're now dead, and nothing else really matters. Please leave the myriad problems of the world to the living."

"But didn't you once visit and meet *Alexander the Great*, and he insisted on granting you any wish you wanted," I hysterically ranted, "and then you absurdly replied, 'Please move out of my sunlight,' and then *Alexander the Great…*"

"Silence!" Diogenes angrily exclaimed as he held his spectral lantern up fully exposing his hideous skeletal face. "Any more outbursts from you will surely result in dire consequences for your captured soul. Heed my simple basic commands Stranger, or else you'll be doomed to a far worse eternal fate than mere death! I trust now that I've concisely communicated that cause-effect relationship to you."

'*I'm* very much like Diogenes, an avowed cynic and a devout skeptic,' I rationally thought. 'Perhaps that is why I'm assigned here and *he* is here. The poor Greek scholar has been commanded to teach *me* what I need to know and what years of doubt could not make me realize,' I conjectured.

My heart felt tempted to mentally ask (for *we* were transmitting thoughts and words through a remarkable telepathy and not by using our mouths and voice-boxes) my distinguished escort if he had ever heard of an Athenian named Socrates but since I didn't desire to antagonize the melancholy morose apparition and subsequently suffer his wrath, I refrained from making the inquiry, for I fathomed that presently *he* had absolute dominion over my weak (and maybe absent) will.

Diogenes led me through the foyer of the shabby antiquated edifice to a gloomy dusty poorly lit lobby and we passed empty chairs with torn upholstery and sofas neglected by time and quite apparently in dire need of repair. At the *Hotel Delaware's* front desk my guide solemnly asked me to sign both my real name "John Wiessner" and my pen name "Jay Dubya" in the ledger, which I cooperatively complied while coincidentally and obediently enacting his baneful command.

"How did you know my real name and how did you know I had a pen name?" I requested knowing. "You must be omniscient," I mentally transmitted.

"Knowledge in this afterlife is transparent and not opaque as it is in *our* former world," Diogenes telepathically related, "and it is not exclusively confined to a person's form or body. I simply read your vulnerable mind as if I was reading an elementary book or a tablet. It's easy once you learn the knack!"

"Well," I commented in sheer amazement, "what about heaven and hell and purgatory and what about everybody else that's dead and *Jesus* and…"

"Look!" my upset escort' said in an admonishing tone of voice, "the information you're requesting is not available or known on this lowly death level. Once you leave this holding area and move on into the greater transcendent afterworld," Diogenes carefully enunciated, "then those questions that riddle your limited comprehension might be satisfactorily answered at the next higher phantom station. Now do you evaluate your lowly status on the eternal ladder?"

"But if I died when my car had veered into the woods," I mentally rebutted, "how could I have lived to put air into my front tire several more times before arriving at the ferry terminal?" I desperately argued. "And Diogenes, if my car was wrecked up and if I was dead on impact, how did I manage to drive it all the way to Cape May to take the ferry across the bay to this horrible *Hotel Delaware?"*

"It probably takes about an earth hour for true death to finally set in," Diogenes theorized and objectively communicated, "and you were still mentally carrying out your trip to the ferry during that delicate hour of transition from your former life to this one. So spiritually, mentally and emotionally," the ancient pessimistic sage cleverly concluded, "you had completed that part of your trip even though your body had perished in the accident you had previously so vividly described."

"Who else is registered here as a guest?" I inquisitively asked. "How many rooms does this place have for occupancy? It looks pre-Victorian in architecture!"

"Please, one appropriate question at a time," Diogenes aggressively chastised. "You have all eternity to learn and decipher what you feel you need to know. You'll discover that the *Hotel Delaware* has thirteen guest rooms. And I don't know if that number is symbolic of anything or not."

I glanced outside a window and the only thing I could discern in the dense fog was the aforementioned unhinged black shutter hanging down from the wooden outside' wall that quite evidently needed several serious heavy coats of paint. "Oh," I thought and communicated, "that symbolism makes a lot of sense having thirteen rooms. Delaware was the first state, and there were thirteen original colonies that had united in the war of independence against England. One room for each colony is a wonderful coincidence! Wouldn't you agree Diogenes?"

I learned from my orientation guide that the other spirit guests residing at the hotel were distinguished personages Benjamin Franklin, George Washington, Thomas Jefferson, Edgar Allan Poe, Abraham Lincoln, Ulysses S. Grant, Mark Twain, Henry Ford, Albert Einstein, Franklin D. Roosevelt, George Herman "Babe" Ruth and Marilyn Monroe.

"But those people are all famous?" I challenged my honorable guide. "What's the meaning of all this? Where do I fit in, a common public school English teacher?"

"You mean they all *were* famous," Diogenes cunningly corrected and clarified.

"But why am I here with all of these deceased celebrities, inventors and presidents if I'm just an unfortunate ordinary dead person?" I demanded knowing. "I certainly lack their accomplishments and their credentials!"

"Maybe you'll become famous after your death just like Herman Melville or William Shakespeare," my ancient Greek ghost page speculated and mentally conveyed. "My senses perceive that you had always wanted to communicate with the dead. Now here's your big chance."

I learned several bizarre things from Diogenes. When Babe Ruth had registered as a guest Christopher Columbus had simultaneously checked out and was moved to another higher plateau in the afterlife. And when Marilyn Monroe's shade was accepted as an official resident, Henry Hudson's apparition was allowed to move on to loftier post mortem pursuits.

"At the rate of new guests and old ones coming and going," I remarked to the stone-faced and generally apathetic Diogenes, "I won't get out of this mediocre *death trap* for another two hundred years judging by how long George Washington has been a visitor here."

"That seems about right," my ghastly-looking skeptical companion agreed. "But you must remember," Diogenes ruefully clarified, "time as you knew it is meaningless at this place. There is little difference between a minute, a day, a century and a millennium at this splendid and unique hotel. Time here can either expand or it can contract. As that fellow Einstein in Room 1955 once told me, everything including time is relative!" my host mentally uttered with a very weak but irritating smile vaguely reflecting from his countenance.

"Oh," I mentally said, "now that makes perfectly good sense. When one person moves in, the lucky spirit that has been here the longest is finally eligible to move out. It's sort of like a predictable rotating lottery of sorts!"

"Right you are Sir," Diogenes aptly concurred with my brilliant deduction. "When you moved in, Ben Franklin, according to the established rotation, must step onto the ferry and be taken to the next station, wherever that is!"

Just then the ferry horns blasted three times, suggesting that Ben Franklin was obediently walking up the ramp and happily departing the dismal dreary grounds and vicinity of the *Hotel Delaware* to embark to some new destination in the very bewildering indefinable death realm.

100

"But why have I been summoned to this morbid death holding station if I'm not famous?" I asked my pale pathetic partner. "I think I really don't deserve to be here! The accomplishments of your other guests certainly eclipse and dwarf mine!"

"Maybe you'll finally have become famous when it's time for your departure on the ferry," my gruesome-looking ghoulish host imaginatively suggested. "Don't short-change yourself, even after you're certifiably dead!"

"I would rather have led a full normal life as a nobody than to sacrifice twenty-five golden years of retirement for fame after my ill-fated automobile accident!" I strenuously objected. "Life is unfair and now I know that death is too!"

My mind (or what was left of it) was in a complete quandary. I asked to be led to my room, which was the only one situated on the hotel's second floor, ironically Number 2004. Then a certain parallel connected inside my confused, befuddled and disoriented mind. The hotel's room numbers corresponded with the exact year each person had perished. I had died in 2004 and I knew from biographical accounts I had read that Dr. Albert Einstein had died in the year 1955.

"Thank you for showing me my living quarters, or should I say my death quarters!" I mentally said to Diogenes. "Are you the only employee here?"

"Why yes," the now guide-turned-butler cerebrally said, still holding his trademark dimly lit lantern. "You'd better keep that exquisite sense of humor of yours," the notorious cynic smartly advised, "because it's guaranteed to raise everyone's *spirits* around here! Ha, ha, ha," he cackled like an obsessed maniac.

"Why do we have to enter and exit via doors if we're spirits?" I seriously asked. "Why don't we just filter through the walls like ghost vapors?"

"We could, but that would be impolite and too annoying to our other guests," Diogenes reprimanded. "It would infringe on their privacy. You wouldn't want that ferry to *barge* into your room would you? Ha, ha, ha," the ancient Greek wildly cackled. "So, George W., Abe L. or Marilyn M. wouldn't enjoy *you* interrupting *their* privacy or their meditation by *your* intrusively whisking your way through the outer wall, would they? I doubt it!" the spirited ghost convincingly argued.

I asked Diogenes to provide me with an abundant supply of pens and writing paper, and to accommodate my requests the specter later rummaged through closets and through desk drawers and eventually located the prescribed items. I thanked my new acquaintance, prudently sat at the dusty desk and assiduously began re-writing my manuscript that I had recently sent to my supportive Annapolis publisher. And after meticulously completing that project', which I thoroughly believed far surpassed the original version in quality, I commenced authoring the first of four prodigious novel-length manuscripts that I had felt inspired to write. 'I have two hundred years to write at my leisure,' I intrepidly surmised, 'and this is one labor of love that I feel compelled to perform. I must organize my novels and novellas as carefully as possible and make each page of superior quality.'

Diogenes had told me that I could export (without penalty) one package into the "physical world" so I was elated when I was able to fill a storage chest with eight thick manuscripts, novels and novella collections. The old chest, loaded to capacity, was then addressed and sent to my publisher in Annapolis', who would be shocked to receive the unanticipated documents authored by a dead writer and surprisingly delivered via conventional parcel post. The details of exactly how this was done or negotiated was never disclosed to me, but I had placed implicit faith and trust in the integrity of the sad-faced Diogenes', who had expertly and expeditiously handled that special favor for me.

It was a very strange existence for me in this morbid but placid afterlife, having no need for either eating or drinking. The desire for biological satisfaction (or for its accompanying pleasures) was totally absent from the two-dimensional death world to which I was confined, but I was happy to note that mental pleasure could still be experienced after I had finished the task of writing those assorted "perfect manuscripts."

Feeling exceptionally lonely, I finally summoned sufficient courage to exit my drab and uninspiring room and visit the eldest guest spirit at the *Hotel Delaware*, so I politely knocked on the door of Room 1799. George Washington graciously answered my knocks and the tall pale specter asked me to enter and review post-colonial history for him.

"It's indeed a distinct honor to meet my country's first President," I began, "and you look identical to your famous portrait that appears on the one dollar bill."

"Sir," the eminent Founding Father and renowned military general said with his mind, "I've never visited anyone else in this confounded hotel. I was afraid that there might be some sort of supernatural reprisal associated with me leaving my humble quarters. Apparently Sir," white-wigged George Washington continued, "you possess great daring to act independently without knowledge of rules and death customs or without fear of consequence."

Then George Washington's specter stated that I too must be a famous person to be confined to the sanctuary of the creepy *Hotel Delaware* even though I was unaware of my fame or reputation by virtue of my untimely and premature departure from mortal existence.

I thanked the venerable American for his unsolicited praise and encouragement and then I learned that all of the books in General Washington's room had been printed *before* 1800. The poor fellow thirsted for knowledge about America after his unfortunate death on December 14, 1799.

"Tell me Sir," the tall powder-wigged giant of history mentally said, "has the *Constitution* and the nation survived the past several hundred years?"

I cogently explained to President Washington all that had transpired from his colonial and *Revolutionary War* era up to the year 2004 including the sensational changes associated with the *Industrial Revolution,* the *Civil War,* the invention of the train and the automobile, the *Great Depression,* the two world wars and the atomic and computer ages. I also divulged that the *Constitution* had been *amended* many times, and we discussed those particular modifications in great length.

"Do you mean to tell me that you own a device you call a car that can go up to sixty miles per hour in just six seconds and you have a special gauge you call a speedometer that registers one hundred and forty miles an hour?" Washington marveled and related. "I guess the stagecoach and the horse and wagon are obsolete. These commentaries of yours are quite astounding! Oh I get it!" Washington exclaimed! "The word automobile means that a coach could move all by itself without any horse pulling it! Quite in-genius if I may add!"

"Well, not exactly," I respectfully clarified. "People still go to race tracks and bet on horse races. A big one is called the *Kentucky Derby.*"

George Washington was fascinated by all that I told him, for we must have exchanged uninterrupted conversation for at least a full earth month without the need of sleep, food or drink. I never thought I could be so vociferous as I had been in *his* inimitable company. And when Washington discovered from our lengthy discourse that there were now fifty states instead of thirteen, his pale face produced a proud broad smile.

President Washington became rather disconsolate upon hearing about the notion of "separation of church and state" and how "the establishment clause" had been "misinterpreted" by a sequence of "unfortunate" *Supreme Court* decisions. "National morality cannot last in exclusion of religious principles," our first chief executive lamented and expressed, "and your public schools should not be devoid of teaching morality based on religious principles either," he mentally elaborated. "Your institutions of learning are therefore producing a vile generation of bratty dolts who might have knowledge in subject matter but who lack discipline, resolve and wisdom that come from the practice of simple basic religious morality. The first *Ten Amendments* to the *Constitution* should be predicated upon the *Ten Commandments* handed down to Moses and embodied in the *Bible,*" George Washington adamantly insisted and emphasized.

I informed my astute listener about abortion rights, about homosexual marriage and about criminal and animal rights. He nearly blew a fuse arguing, "It's a travesty to believe that such ungodly things have been resulting from the misguided interpretation of a Godly-inspired document such as the sacred *United States Constitution*. And when you tell me that God has been taken out of your public schools," Washington continued in an emotional state that bordered rage, "then I believe that I had fought the entire *Revolutionary War* in vain. Our nation is doomed to decay from within. Civil rights will ultimately destroy individual morality, which will produce the decadence that will weaken and then eventually erode away the foundational values of *our* great nation. There is no doubt in my mind that that catastrophic end will be inevitable!"

On the optimistic side, the first President was elated to know that the country had survived over two centuries of critical challenges since his death in 1799. The great statesman and military strategist found hope in the prospect that a national crisis similar to the *Civil War* or the *Great Depression* might once again shake the country out of apathy after the year 2004. George Washington's spirit explicitly indicated to me that there possibly would emerge a noble crusade to return to the great moral roots and the powerful American traditions strongly embodied in the *Declaration of Independence* and in the *Bill of Rights*. He referred to this phenomenon as "the Phoenix resurrection."

Upon leaving the General's "solitary confinement sanctuary," George Washington's ghost thanked me for my informative visit while regretting that I had conveyed some "distasteful news" about future events and changes in the "established moral codes" that have been over the years erroneously affected by judicial and legislative adaptations in the "legal codes."

I left George Washington's humble accommodations at the singular *Hotel Delaware* and returned to my own morgue-like second floor room. It again occurred to me that since I had died in the year 2004, I had the only *death quarters* on the second tier. Then an interesting thought flashed through my transparent brain. When additional renowned people would die, more second-floor rooms would have to be added on to the ancient hotel so that the new restless spirits could peacefully dwell until they were allowed to ascend to the next dreadful echelon in the afterlife. 'Or perhaps there are many other death holding stations similar to this *Hotel Delaware* to allow for the other decedents,' I hypothesized.

I stayed dormant in my room for an unspecified interval of time, which to my comprehension remained quite anonymous and mysterious because there were no clocks or wristwatches or views of the sun and the moon from anywhere inside the dreary deplorable hotel. Then I attempted to prepare the outline to a new manuscript but ideas and words eluded me, so I temporarily abandoned that ambitious enterprise.

I decided I would pay a visit to another extraordinary personage trapped in the archaic weather-worn domicile, so I elected to interact with a particular idol of mine from nineteenth century American literature. I had to choose between Edgar Allan Poe and Mark Twain. I chose the former hoping to have an opportunity to speak with Samuel Langhorne Clemens at a future date (even though calendars and dates did not exist anywhere inside the very weird and obscure hotel).

My knuckles rapped on the door of Room 1849 and mused that Edgar Allan Poe would assume that I was an itinerant raven determined to annoy and pester him, all relaxed in *his* tranquil solitude.

"Hello," I greeted the literary master. "May I come in to chat for a while?"

"Certainly," Poe cooperatively replied. "You look harmless although I must laugh at the strange apparel ornamenting your body. I presume you are from a future age? You appear too casual to be dead. Is that how you were buried? Has formality been abandoned entirely?"

"No Sir, er I mean, I don't think I was ever buried and have no knowledge of being buried," I stammered. "This is what I was wearing when I died."

"Well then," my illustrious academic erudite host persisted, "are you from *my* future?"

"Yes Sir," I keenly answered the much-revered genius. "You happen to be a favorite author of mine and I immensely enjoyed teaching my students many of your fine stories," I sincerely elaborated. "I was a school teacher during most of my life," I clarified, "and your tales of horror and your classic adventure stories were among the best I ever read or analyzed. I especially liked teaching my students your tales 'The Cask of Amontillado' and 'The Fall of the House of Usher'."

Poe was quite flattered by my complimentary remarks and asked me to sit down even though I no longer possessed a body that required rest from its weight or from its exertion. I honored my literary benefactor's request out of force of habit and out of respect for past human courtesy customs.

"Well kind Sir," E.A. began, "you must know about my dear Virginia?"

"Your wife Virginia died of tuberculosis in 1847, so in all due deference," I said, "you know more about her last moments on earth than I do since you passed away in 1849."

"I apologize, kind Sir," Edgar Allan Poe mentally transmitted momentarily exhibiting a rare smile, "but I originally meant the state of Virginia where I grew up and whose memory I have always held dearly inside my miserable heart."

And after I educated Edgar Allan that there were now forty-nine states in the Union besides his precious Virginia, the cheeks on the pale ghost's countenance almost turned from ashen to pink. He had accurately speculated that a bloody forthcoming *Civil War* was imminent after 1849, but a tear seemed to form in his right eye when I explained the tragedy and the widespread suffering in both the American North and the Dixie South. Many painful wounds had to be healed after the devastating conflict between the *Union* and the *Confederacy.* "A period of *Reconstruction* had to be initiated," I very patiently explained. My listener was just as glad as George Washington had been about the acquisition of additional states to the *Union.*

I immediately identified with the dead man's unique sense of patriotism and with his skeptical outlook on death and its eternal idleness. Much to my surprise, Edgar Allan Poe was amazed that he would become a famous giant in American literature after his untimely death in 1849. The master of the macabre had been found lying outside a Baltimore voting place on October 3 of that year, and he had died in a hospital four days later without ever regaining consciousness.

"Do you mean to say that my work is read in virtually every high school and college English class in the country?" Poe incredulously mentally asked and marveled. "I knew I would die in poverty and disgrace," he bluntly continued with remorse and disenchantment, "but I never reckoned I would achieve national and international acclaim. You Sir, pardon my aggressive nomenclature," E.A. paused to measure my reaction, "are a most welcomed time courier. In you I see much of me, and I mean this with sincerity when I say that it is most grievously calamitous that you too are deceased and doomed to incarceration in this lackluster hotel. Have you attained notoriety during your lifetime?"

"No," I lamented, "and I really don't know why I've been assigned to and imprisoned here in the *Hotel Delaware* with such a distinguished group of literary, famous and historical souls occupying the other rooms."

"Perhaps you too will be visited by a messenger rapping on your door several hundred years from now and told of your great contributions to civilization," Poe theorized and suggested. "Then *you* will know the pure pristine genuine delight I'm presently feeling at learning that my life's work has achieved honor and prestige in the literary community, a community that vehemently abhorred me and my endeavors and one that I absolutely despised and loathed during my brief tenure on the earth."

Then I had the pleasure of discussing with the master most of his outstanding literary gems including "The Cask of

Amontillado," "Murders in the Rue Morgue," "The Fall of the House of Usher," "The Tell-Tale Heart," "The Black Cat," "The Pit and the Pendulum" and the "Masque of the Red Death." I was *literally* held spellbound and was thoroughly captivated by Poe's vivid animated descriptions and by his graphic explanations in regard to what critics consider his classic works.

In "The Purloined Letter," I curiously stated, "you had essentially invented the entire theory and methodology of the detective story," I praised the great short story author, "and thousands of writers since your time have imitated the excellent model that you've so effectively pioneered. I believe," I respectfully continued, "that you Sir, and I sincerely mean this, have been perhaps the greatest influence on the course of American literature over the past two centuries."

"I always believed that the ideal critic should be objective while slightly leaning toward the negative side," Poe declared while alluding to his literary reputation at being a premiere reviewer of essays and short stories. "So that's why I get along so well with Diogenes," he humorously added. "But above all else an author must possess originality, courage of heart and the grammatical skill to efficiently convey *his* message to his readers. Otherwise," the disconsolate and totally bored fellow decided, "the author is not an author at all but merely a very ambitious writer aspiring to great accomplishments but doomed to failure or be destined to produce mediocrity."

I had fathomed and found much merit in Edgar Allan Poe's enlightening commentaries and I only wished at that moment that I could return to my human form and pursue my literary aspirations with the superb knowledge I had absorbed during our most intriguing dialogue. When neither of us had anything additional to relate or to discuss, I bid the prolific genius possessing a burgeoning vocabulary "adieu" and next shuffled down the dank dim corridor and then climbed up the rickety steps back to my non-inspirational room.

My consciousness was gratified by the keen insights that the eminent editorial authority had to share with one of *his* humble admirers. Poe's final words remained in my mind and after the comprehensive interview my brain tended to review them incessantly. "Always remember kind Sir," the literary master imperatively transmitted, "a combination of truth, soul, passion, beauty and creativity is what elevates literature to a higher shelf than the one occupied by mundane newspaper journalism and by ridiculous written political propaganda."

Throughout my humble life I, like Edgar Allan Poe, tended to be reclusive and moody. I never really liked gossip, small talk or was fascinated by glib and garrulous people. 'An introverted nature was also an introspective advantage that both Poe and I cherished and exercised during *our* separate writing sessions,' I realized. "We both like to be alone to ponder and to explore our inner souls and to investigate the deepest secrets lying within our hearts,' I then understood. 'We both loathed obnoxious and ultra-gregarious people.'

And soon a much more enlightening theory entered my troubled mind. I was in one way or another much like all of the inhabitants of the deteriorating un-maintained *Hotel Delaware*. I was diplomatic and gentlemanly like Washington, introverted and emotionally tormented like Poe, and inventive with an *Alpha* (aggressive and determined) personality like Thomas Alva Edison, whom I had selected to be my next hotel resident to interview.

I had by then accepted my possible two-hundred-year confinement in the gloomy *Hotel Delaware* in a rather stoical manner, and then I finally became cognizant of another interesting facet of the complex mystic puzzle. I was also very much like Diogenes, priding myself on being a skeptic and a cynic about most everything and most anything.

I confidently descended the decrepit staircase to the ground-level corridor and floated (without walking a single step) down to Room 1931 where Thomas Alva Edison's spirit was quietly kept to ruminate. The man's *shade* was a little hard of hearing but after I had introduced myself in a loud clear voice, Edison welcomed me into his disheveled room that had so many cobwebs that it reminded me of a monstrous cocoon. That notion immediately made me contemplate that *we* were indeed trapped in some sort of indefinable chrysalis, waiting to be released into a new existence just as an ugly caterpillar transforms into a beautiful butterfly inside a second *natural* womb.

"I must say I admire your audacity," Edison's ghost remarked as it eagerly greeted me at *his* door. "You demonstrate the daring of an old friend of mine, Henry Ford," he praised. "Make yourself comfortable if that's at all possible in this bizarre rudimentary plateau in the afterlife."

"Why Henry Ford!" I exclaimed in a very un-ghostly-like manner. "He's staying in this same hotel in Room 1947. I remember his name and room number from the registry ledger kept down in the main lobby."

"Why I'll be giraffe's grandfather!" Thomas A. Edison bellowed in an uncharacteristic and excessive display of emotion. "I've been staying here at this repugnant run-down hotel right down the hall from one of my favorite contemporaries and completely ignorant of that fact until *you* came along and informed me. I'll have to garner up enough gumption to mimic your fine example and pay the old coot a surprise visit!"

Edison was very anxious to know what had transpired in the world after 1931, and upon hearing about *Bose* sound systems, computer floppy and compact disks, video cassettes, color television, cell phones and the *Internet*, the great inventor' who possessed over a thousand United States' patents heartily and exuberantly laughed out loud.

"You know," the incomparable genius Thomas Edison responded, "I only wish that I could've lived to see in full operation all that you've so admirably described. I'm so glad and proud that my years of research and experimentation had led to the discovery of these phenomenal creations that you've so wonderfully related," the ingenious fellow mentally said and savored. "Your news has brought joy to my heart and peace to my restless soul!"

"Yes," I matter-of-factly added, "and there are high schools, towns and townships named after you all over the United States," I congratulated, "and believe it or not you're still affectionately referred to as the *Wizard of Menlo Park*. And your famous statement 'A genius is one tenth inspiration and nine tenths perspiration' is widely quoted all the time all over the modern world," I complimented.

"Allow me to modify that if I may," Edison insisted. "It ought to be 'A genius is one-third inspiration, one-third perspiration and one- third desperation!" the great contributor to science and technology aptly joked. "If only I could return to my laboratory in Menlo Park for just one earthly minute! That would be a terrific moment I would definitely cherish for all eternity!"

Thomas A. Edison and I conversed for the longest time and reviewed just about everything from stereo radios to space satellite communications. Throughout our extended dialogue, the

110

wrinkle-faced man was again a human dynamo exhibiting a great *spirit* and a youthful enthusiasm for all subjects our imaginations touched upon. And when the accomplished inventor heard that his New Jersey research laboratory' had been proclaimed a treasured national monument by President Dwight D. Eisenhower in 1956, Edison's sunken eyes seemed to illuminate and his mental articulation became most jubilant.

"You are indeed a Godsend," the creative guru triumphantly declared in appreciation of the intellectual stimulation our conference had provided. "I'm deeply indebted to you for verifying that my life's work has been worthwhile. I now feel that I had laid the foundations for the discovery of more intricate and sophisticated appliances and devices that'll most certainly be beneficial to mankind," the gray-faced spirit gleefully announced. "You have definitely *made my century!*"

Edison and I must have talked for at least several more earth months without any trace of exhaustion evident in the rhetoric of either of us. Finally, after informing my prestigious host all about the capabilities of the *Hubble Space Telescope* and all about exploratory interplanetary probes to Mars and Jupiter, I left the highly esteemed inventor's company and returned to the quiet sanctuary of my shadowy second floor room.

Several more months must have elapsed before I decided to exit my "dying quarters," slowly amble down to the dark and dreary lobby and initiate a conversation with the sometimes' talkative but moody sage Diogenes.

"Well Diogenes," I cunningly began, "I have had the pleasure of meeting the ghosts of George Washington, Edgar Allan Poe and Thomas Edison. Now I can't wait to mingle with Thomas Jefferson, Abraham Lincoln, Mark Twain, Ulysses S. Grant, Albert Einstein, Henry Ford and Marilyn Monroe, if I accurately recall all of the other hotel spectral guests."

"Kind Sir," Diogenes answered, "please examine the new names listed in the register. I believe almost two centuries have expired in the outside world since your arrival, and now I suspect that *you* are now the senior resident of the *Hotel Delaware.*"

I gazed down at the ledger situated on the dusty registration desk and saw that all of the honorable names I had just enumerated were gone from the list. Instead were unfamiliar appellations such as Sir Hiram Applebee, Salvatore Giovanni,

Mildred Carson, Thomas Attanasi, Roseann Celia, Gerald Gares, Arthur Orsi and William Burns.

"Who are these people?" I uttered in sheer protest. "I never heard of any of them! They must all be pedestrian commoners!"

"They are inventors, presidents and entertainers that have become famous during *your* relaxing two-century stay at the *Hotel Delaware!*" Diogenes academically lectured quite nonchalantly. "However, they will certainly recognize your name since your glorious fame has certainly preceded theirs!"

"Do you mean it's already time for me to be transferred to a more enlightening holding area somewhere else in the afterlife?" I sadly asked my aged and withered friend. "I thought I heard the ferry's foghorns several times but I was so engrossed in meditating in my room that I never looked out the window into the dense fog or stepped downstairs to investigate it's arrival," I reported to Diogenes in a melancholy tone of voice.

Just then the ferry's whistle blasted three times and I instinctively knew that a new hotel occupant was about to come ashore. Diogenes left me standing in the dingy lobby, and several minutes later the scary-looking apparition reappeared alongside a middle-age spirit still attempting to decipher and define his new gloomy surroundings.

"Hello," I said to the new *Hotel Delaware* guest standing next to me in the dark and dreary lobby. "My name is John Wiessner and I'm glad to meet you!"

"John Wiessner!" the fellow gasped in astonishment. "You mean John Wiessner, alias Jay Dubya! Why you're my favorite author! I've read all of your short stories, *Hammonton Gazette* opinion columns, all of your novellas and all of your novels. This is indeed the highlight of my death experience!"

"And who might you be?" I inquired. "Certainly you must be famous to be invited as a welcomed guest at this temporary holding platform."

"My name is Jason Parsons," the dead fellow's ghost mentally stated, "and I perfected and invented the *Babel Universal Communicator* in 2154."

"What does it do?" I insisted on knowing. "Does it communicate with other planets in the *Milky Way?*"

"*The Babel Universal Communicator* is a handheld computer device that enables people of different languages to communicate the brain pulses of their thought patterns in *their* language into

112

the words and sentences of a person speaking another language, no matter what it is," Jason Parsons eagerly explained. "A voice simulator I had developed and patented translates the words through a powerful micro-speaker into the second language so that two people of different nationalities or cultures could easily hold an intelligent extensive conversation upon first contact."

"Wow!" I exclaimed with great admiration. "Babel then refers to the *Biblical Tower of Babel* where everyone in the Babylon area suddenly spoke different languages. Jason Parsons, I'm very glad to make your acquaintance," I sincerely said, "and don't worry about a thing. Your stay at the *Hotel Delaware* will be both rewarding and soon completed before you know it if you know how to use your time constructively and wisely. Now tell me, how did you happen to die?"

"I think my wife poisoned me when she found out I was having an affair with a beautiful and voluptuous *Hollywood* movie star," Jason Parsons revealed. "But I'm not sure if jealousy was her real motive or whether she simply wanted to inherit my fortune because she was having extra-curricular affairs with the gardener and the chauffeur. At any rate," Jason finished with a degree of anguish and distress, "I'm damned dead now and I don't give a Marley's or a Great Caesar's Ghost about it. I just feel extremely betrayed, that's all."

"Women led to *your* demise," Diogenes concluded and insisted as he held *his* dimly lit lantern up to Jason Parsons' honest-looking face. "Both the woman that you desired and the woman that you had have contributed to your eternal fate!"

Then I heard the ferry horn blast three additional times, signaling its intent of disembarking from its mooring and venturing out into the thick *Delaware Bay* fog to the second level of enlightenment and emotional growth in the peculiar-but-fascinating vertical death tier hierarchy.

"Maybe now I'll find out about heaven, hell and Jesus and everything else, " I said to Diogenes and to Jason Parsons. "I'm now fully prepared to deal with the attendant duties and responsibilities of the next level of spiritual growth, whatever those details might entail!"

Diogenes escorted me to the *Hotel Delaware's* lobby door. I warmly shook his cold numb hand, stepped out of the macabre dilapidated structure, descended the thirteen rickety steps and hastened through the dense fog to the ferry. I triumphantly ascended the entrance ramp with all the vigor that a veteran ghost could muster. I had no apprehension about or fear of my next surreal destination.

I then understood that I was mentally equipped and emotionally mature to adequately deal with the elements that awaited me on death's enigmatic second stage of existence. I intuitively also now fully understand that Diogenes had successfully shipped the wooden chest of manuscripts into the past via some wonderful alien method of time compression. I now thoroughly comprehend and appreciate a third significant truth. I had become Jay Dubya's anonymous *ghostwriter* during my memorable two-century hiatus at the *Hotel Delaware*.

I'm placing this manuscript describing my death experiences in an empty five-gallon plastic spring water bottle I've found on the deserted ferry. And after inserting the cork tightly in the bottle's neck, I'll toss the container overboard hoping that some lucky mortal will find it and have a brief glimpse of the spirit world awaiting him or her.

"The Better of Two Lives"

People make many crucial decisions from several years after womb right up to tomb. Men and women usually encounter at least a dozen crossroad events in their lifetimes where important choices are made, some good, and perhaps some not so fortuitous as originally planned and hoped for. Major decisions about marriage, who to marry, career choice, real estate acquisitions and investments complement a person's numerous minor preferences in addition to which sports to play, who to ask to the senior prom, which college to attend and what kind of house should be purchased. Such a plethora of mental challenges affect millions of Americans daily and throughout their mortal lives.

Richard Henderson was no exception to the law of human choices. The jack-of-all-trades and master of none had always desired to become a successful businessman, a renowned author and a devoted husband to a wife that fully believed in emotional reciprocity. Those noble aspirations represented Henderson's wishful goals and lofty ambitions, but quite often, obtained results seldom match the sincerity of initial intent. Richard Henderson's youthful fantasy and idealism rapidly deteriorated into shattered hopes and crushed dreams.

Approaching age sixty, Richard critically evaluated his life's lackluster accomplishments. His assessment led to feelings of guilt, depression and frustration. The despondent man had not achieved what he had set out to attain, even though he had always given his efforts "the old college try." Rather than seek professional counseling, Henderson allowed his sense of futility to govern his mental and emotional health. Dejection and despair dominated Richard's heart, mind and spirit.

On the morning of April 24th, 2002, Richard Henderson climbed into his brand-new leased red-colored *Toyota Avalon*. He pressed the automatic portal's remote control, exited one of two garage doors leading into his two-story white colonial home, methodically closed the enclosure and then turned left out of his U-shaped driveway onto the *White Horse Pike*.

'Things haven't exactly turned out the way I had expected,' the driver thought as he passed *by Oak Grove Cemetery* on his short excursion into Hammonton, a somnolent agricultural community in southern New Jersey famous for its summer blueberry crop. 'It's Jennifer's and my thirty-sixth wedding anniversary,' the driver lamented as he accelerated past a cement truck, which was en route to the new high school construction site across Old Forks Road from the cemetery. 'If only things had worked out differently, or should I be thinking worked out better,' the man regretted. 'Oh well, it's now all water over the proverbial dam!'

A dominant disheartened disposition ruled Richard's mind as he steered his sleek swift automobile onto Bellevue Avenue, Hammonton's main thoroughfare. Henderson's fertile imagination assessed the past three and a half decades of his undistinguished life, his mind wishing that he had made other choices in those ever-present "*old forks* in the road," and then wondering and speculating what outcomes would have culminated from alternative paths he might have taken.

"I'm worth more dead than alive," the disgruntled fellow muttered to his middle-age appearance in the car's rear-view mirror. 'The only tangible thing I have to show for thirty-six years of labor is a house without a mortgage,' Richard mentally reviewed with regret. Then a passing thought tinkered with the driver's better judgment. 'If I kill myself by smashing into a tree or a telephone pole, Jennifer and the kids could collect the balance of my pension. I have three hundred thousand dollars remaining in my pension account, and if I suddenly disappear from this dog-eat-dog earth, then at least my wife and kids will be able to receive a half-decent estate when you throw into the mix my quarter million dollar accidental death insurance policy. I don't know why it's called life insurance if it exclusively involves death. I suppose that's one of those euphemisms that glib television commentators talk about all the time.'

Richard's daydreaming' was terminated as he perceived flashing red lights up ahead and then noticed the Bellevue Avenue railroad crossing gates descending. As he restlessly waited for the *New Jersey Transit Express* from Atlantic City to Lindenwold to swiftly pass through downtown Hammonton, Henderson's mind rekindled several of its latest warped suppositions. 'I draw thirty thousand dollars a year out of my pension,' Richard recalled and theorized, 'and I'm still four years away from collecting social security. That's another eleven thousand a year. A motley forty-one thousand dollar total retirement package. What a wasted life!'

The *New Jersey Transit Express* train whizzed by, the Bellevue Avenue gates ascended back to their vertical positions and traffic again crossed the landmark railroad tracks. Instead of stopping at his primary destination, a popular town convenience store, Richard forgot about his morning newspaper and doughnuts and coffee and progressed straight down Bellevue Avenue, which then became Twelfth Street and finally a mile further south the road transformed into State Highway *Route 54.*

'I've valiantly tried, but I've failed over and over again!' the mentally disturbed man concluded. 'My marriage and my career haven't quite turned out as I had planned. I've been rejected and been a failure much more than I can cope with. I should've never become an English teacher for thirty-four years of sacrifice and student discipline problems. I could've gone into business many times, but always foolishly put family needs first. And where has it gotten me? To the brink of insanity, that's where!' the emotionally distressed driver generalized.

As the merlot-color *Toyota Avalon* left the town limits, the state road expanded from two lanes to a four-lane dual highway. The retired English instructor expressed his emotional dissatisfaction by mashing his right foot against the accelerator. The auto's speedometer was now registering sixty-five miles per hour. Tears formed in the anguished driver's eyes and several rolled down his cheeks. Richard reflexively wiped the excessive dampness away from under his bifocals.

'I could've bought my parents' farm market,' the distraught fellow recalled, 'and I could've married my college sweetheart Carolyn Williams instead of hitching up with Jennifer Ranere. I could've bought several boardwalk businesses in Ocean City, Maryland, and I should've invested in gold during the seventies oil crisis. Could have, would have, should have!' Richard angrily hypothesized. 'That's the story of my hapless life! One continuous pattern of inaction!'

The disconsolate man glanced below the dashboard at the speedometer, which now indicated eighty miles an hour. 'And I tried turning things around,' Henderson regretted and sobbed. 'I borrowed heavily on my credit cards, raising them to their limits, accumulating thirty thousand dollars debt to e-publish my ten novels. My *Internet* web sites have gotten over a hundred thousand hits but it's just like owning a gift shop getting thousands of browsers but no paying customers. What a horrific nightmare my life's biography is! A complete financial disaster!'

The speeder was becoming more and more delirious as he unfortunately passed a state police car while doing ninety miles an hour. Immediately the red flashing lights on the state trooper's roof illuminated as the officer initiated his hot pursuit. Richard stared into the rear view mirror and observed the cop trailing *his* exceptionally fast 255 horsepower automobile.

'I can't take it anymore!' Richard thought as he put the pedal to the metal. The speedometer was now reading a hundred miles an hour and Richard wondered if he could get the vehicle up to the maximum 160 miles an hour position. "Sold only two dozen books on the *Internet!*" he screamed. "Not even my friends and family have bought any of my books!" Richard shrieked as if he were an obsessed maniac. "Nobody cares about me, absolutely nobody!" the inconsolable man yelled at his rear-view mirror.

The merlot *Toyota Avalon* swerved back and forth, weaving from lane to lane, and then the out-of-control machine just missed having a head-on collision with an oncoming tractor-trailer as the highway bottlenecked down to two-lanes again. The driver of the diesel eighteen-wheeler was blasting his air-horn as the red *Toyota* zoomed past. The fancy sports car veered off *Highway 54* and quickly crashed into a small cluster of evergreen trees, collapsing from the tremendous impact like a compressed accordion.

'I refuse to be doomed to dismal mediocrity! I would rather die!' were Richard's final contemplations before lapsing into unconsciousness.

A fantasy of bright lights and blinking colors prevailed around the accident scene and then for Richard Henderson a high velocity entrance into a narrow dark tunnel with his spiritual existence heading towards the glimmering and shimmering sparkles. Soon Richard's perception became aware of his body experiencing a floating sensation as the man was hovering over his corpse lying on the ground next to his demolished *Avalon.* The state trooper and a team of paramedics were frantically administering *CPR* to his lifeless form, and then after that attempt had failed the men were futilely trying to revive *his* vital signs with the implementation of a portable defibrillator.

'At last, it's over. Instantly and painlessly over!' Richard marveled at how ingeniously easy it had been to die. 'If I had to do it all over again that's exactly the method I would use!'

"That's what you think!" said a winged figure clad in a white silk gown. "Richard Henderson, that's what you think! You ought to be ashamed of your cowardly suicide act!"

"Who are you?" the semi-dead fugitive from life asked the bothersome angel.

"I'm your conscience, possibly your guilty conscience," the celestial being emphatically answered. "You have wished you could have made other more fruitful choices in your life that would've guaranteed you certain material rewards. You've relentlessly complained that you've dedicated your adult life to the betterment of your students Richard Henderson, and I must give you ample credit, indeed you have. *The Greater Power* has assigned me to give you the opportunity to alter your final unwise choice, which was to end your mortal existence," the radiant winged being explained. "This pardon has only been conferred because you, Richard Henderson, have selflessly given of yourself helping over four thousand children master the mechanics of English grammar and the development of a certain love for literature. Otherwise your mortal sin violation would never have been reviewed."

Richard Henderson stared fifty feet down at his motionless body lying on the damp ground, the medical personnel and the police officer completely unaware of *his* or the benevolent angel's overhead spiritual presence.

"Now Richard, you shall accompany me through a half century of space and time, to a simpler period, your post high school years," the magnificent creature predicted. "I suggest that you relax and enjoy your brief excursion into your past!"

The angel whisked its right hand and almost instantaneously Richard was enveloped in a swirling whirlwind, more like the benign eye of a hurricane than a violent tempest. When the revolving clouds and the accompanying eddying haze gradually vanished, the astounded mortal was shown a memorable and nostalgic depiction by his heavenly ambassador.

"Does this scenario ring a bell from your past?" the most excellent angel rhetorically asked. "It ought to Richard Henderson! You had an opportunity to purchase your parents' place of business," the angel aptly declared.

Richard Henderson eavesdropped on a conversation that was taking place around an all-too-familiar dining room table. His parents were seated at either end, begging their eldest son to buy the family roadside farm market.

"Rich, your father has suffered a damaging heart attack," Martha Henderson declared, "and the doctors say that the next one could be fatal. Your father and I have decided to sell our business but we'd like to offer you the first chance to acquire it."

"That's right son," Jack Henderson agreed and verified. "Your mother and I have decided to make you a worthy proposition. Buy the farm market from us for forty-thousand-dollars," Mr. Henderson pleaded. "You could have the best of both worlds. Teach school and put up with the board of education and your administrators' demands for nine months and then enjoy being an independent self-employed businessman during the summertime."

"But Dad, I don't want to go into debt and carry a heavy mortgage for the next ten years. I plan on marrying Jennifer Ranere next spring and will need money for a diamond ring and a down payment on a first house," Richard all-too-candidly replied without giving the matter a second thought. "And besides, I think that Jen's father is going to eventually give me a high position in his furniture store business."

"Okay son, if that's what you want," Mr. Jack Henderson sadly answered. "Your mother and I were just thinking about keeping the fruit and vegetable market in the family before selling it to strangers, that's all. We wanted to give you first preference but now your mother and I know your negative position on the subject."

"Thanks Dad. I appreciate your concern and your offer," Richard sincerely stated, "but right now I see more opportunity and more potential for advancement in the furniture business. And if *that* prospect falls through, I'll always have teaching to rely on."

Richard stared directly into the guardian angel's radiant blue eyes. "But I've often wondered what would've happened if I had bought the farm market from Dad and Mom," the temporarily resurrected dead human inquired to his sage guide. "Would that have been the proper decision? I think so, but I'm still unsure right up to this very minute!"

"Nothing ventured, nothing gained or lost," the angel logically commented while waving his right hand, erasing the family dining room scene and replacing it with another familiar tableau that was still coming into focus.

"Could you be more specific?" Richard inquired. "I need to know what would've happened if I had gone into debt and purchased the farm market."

"If you had acquired the premises for forty-thousand dollars, your loving parents would not have charged you any interest on the principal amount," the heavenly creature revealed. "Four years later you could've sold the property four sixty-thousand dollars, and counting your twenty-five thousand dollar equity in the business, you could've amassed a stellar forty-five thousand dollar profit, which in 1970s money converted into today's figures would be a whopping four-hundred thousand dollars. What do you have to say for yourself now?"

"I now realize *that* was a huge mistake I had selfishly made," Richard Henderson acknowledged and shared with the angel. "I should've listened to my parents and heeded their judicious advice about Mr. James Ranere and the furniture business. The grass is always greener…"

"And the furniture polish is always shinier on the other side," the clever angel amusingly finished. "And in the spring of 1966, April 24th to be precise, you had married Jennifer Ranere at St. Joseph Church on North Third Street."

"Against her father's wishes," Richard admitted with a frown. "I now understand that it's a mistake for a man to marry someone above his social status. I was too naive and immature to make that judgment when I was a foolish young man. Mr. Ranere rejected me' and my personal ambition concerning the furniture store right from the start. But as I've already said Angel, I was too young and unsuspecting to catch on at first."

The seemingly omniscient angel once more motioned his right hand and then miraculously several showroom displays of a large furniture store appeared before their eyes. "You believed back in 1966 that you and Jennifer were both teachers and could make a comfortable living with you being employed in her father's reputable store during the summer months, didn't you Richard Henderson?" the beautiful graceful being asked its ward.

"That's right," Richard candidly agreed staring at his guide's brilliant spectrum-hued halo, "and I was sure that I could've made a valuable contribution to my father-in-law's prosperous enterprise. But Jennifer was unhappy and fully stressed-out over teaching kindergarten after thirteen tough years and then she handed-in her resignation. Her father hired her as a record-keeper working in the store's office."

"And in the meantime, Jennifer and you had the first of three sons," the glowing angel interrupted, "and you were sensitive about Mr. James Ranere incessantly picking on you and treating you meanly if not cruelly."

"Your statements are true and accurate," Henderson concurred nodding his head, "and while I was supposed to be in charge of the retail department, my father-in-law made me deliver all of the furniture to customers' houses, often all by myself. And then when he put me in charge of the shipping department," Richard rankled and cringed, "I still had to deliver all of the furniture to customers' houses like a common flunky laborer. Jennifer's old man really put the screws to me good."

The angel summarized and orally conveyed that Mr. Ranere was determined to break-up his oldest daughter's marriage so that Richard Henderson was thwarted from cashing-in on any future lucrative inheritance and from operating the profitable furniture store. "You were given a salary that amounted to a mere dollar above minimum wage," the magnificent creature reminded Henderson, "and your paltry bonus came to only two thousand dollars a year. That was a pittance even by 1966 standards!"

"And my wife was under instructions from her father that I had to pay all of the family bills including house mortgage, insurances, utilities, property taxes and vacations," Richard argued in defense of himself. "I was never able to save anything, while Mr. Ranere advanced his loyal spoiled-rotten daughter thousands of dollars annually under the table. All of that just to spite our relationship and to curry loyalty from Jennifer! My wife and kids always had money while I had to struggle and sweat simply to make ends meet. They were favored, and I was disfavored as the intrusive avaricious outsider!" Henderson grieved.

The radiant angel then reminded Richard that *he* had dated another pretty girl in college, an attractive co-ed named Carolyn Williams, a beauty pageant contestant who had won the distinction of *Miss Brigantine*. When Richard imagined what would have transpired if he had married Carolyn Williams instead of Jennifer Ranere, the omnipotent escort intercepted the mortal's mental transmission and immediately related to the essence of Henderson's conjecture.

"Brigantine is such a pleasant and cozy resort town just above Atlantic City," the clairvoyant creature articulated. The magnificent being then waved his magical right hand, eliminating the disturbing furniture store scenario and adroitly substituting a Jersey shore funeral parlor in its stead. "You attended Carolyn's father's viewing," the angel alertly and perceptively stated.

"That is correct," Richard confessed with a trace of remorse evident in his quivering voice, "but Jennifer went with me and stayed in the car. Just two weeks before Mr. Williams' death Jennifer had made me promise her that I would not see Carolyn any more or else *our* relationship would have been through. I should've known right then and there that Jennifer Ranere's demand was a flagrant red flag warning for future conflict and power struggles between *us* and between her father and me."

And then the splendid angel made Henderson recollect how *he* often had violent disputes with Mr. James Ranere. One day the son-in-law had left the furniture store in a huff and drove down to Ocean City, Maryland where a fellow teacher had a summer job managing a boardwalk amusement arcade.

"My friend hired me on the spot as the assistant manager for a hundred fifty dollars a week," Richard reminisced and confided to the angel (who already knew the entire story), "and right then and there my good buddy offered to share his two bedroom apartment so that I could live rent free."

"And in 1967 you gave Jennifer an ultimatum," the guardian angel injected and reminded Richard. "That action did require a degree of courage on your part. You said, 'Either' come down to Maryland and live in the apartment with the baby or else our flimsy marriage is doomed to divorce'."

The angel and the mortal next discussed how Jennifer had conceded and had brought baby Jimmy to Ocean City, Maryland to also live with the helpful teacher/arcade manager/friend and *his* wife. The following summer Richard had borrowed money from his parents and grandparents and became a partner in the aforementioned boardwalk amusement arcade, and Henderson operated the establishment from 1968-'81 until it was knocked out of business by a Gaming Device Tax imposed retroactively by the heartless *Internal Revenue Service.*

"That's right," Richard remembered and confirmed, "they wanted to make the gaming device tax retroactive for from 1968-1981, the lousy year that the *IRS* made the outrageous claim against my business. The government had actually knocked me out of business maintaining that thirty poker machines I had owned were gaming devices operating by *chance* when actually they were amusement devices operating by the *skill* and the eye-hand coordination of the players," Henderson recollected and described to the angel. "But I had to prove the wretched government wrong, and the greedy lawyers I had to compensate for their top shelf' services, which amounted to another enormous expense in addition to the unwarranted federal tax, penalties and interest that had accumulated. I didn't know who the bigger crooks were, the ruthless *IRS* agents or the vulture lawyers! One was worse than the other!"

"Here's exactly what would have happened if you had married Carolyn Williams instead of linking up with Jennifer Ranere," the angel objectively remarked as he gestured his hand and changed several shadows into female characters present and standing in the Ocean City, Maryland boardwalk arcade tableau.

"Wow! I'm now married to Carolyn and I still have the Ocean City, Maryland business going. The year must be around 1968, and we both seem very happy," Richard rejoiced upon viewing the new set of circumstances.

"Happiness, just like human existence is very temporal and most ephemeral," the empathetic angel intelligently indicated. "Carolyn would've been very supportive of you until around mid-1974. Right after your dad passed away from a massive heart seizure, your wife Carolyn would have begun practicing infidelity. You stayed the course, however, and in this alternate existence you lucked out by selling your thriving boardwalk business for two hundred thousand dollars," the angel divulged to the astonished listener. "That all happened in 1975, a year before *your* unfortunate sale victim that had purchased your arcade paid you that handsome sum. Then the heartless *IRS* knocked him and his partners out of business instead of you."

"Oh my God!" Richard slapped his face in recognition of what would have transpired if he had married Carolyn Williams.

"Kindly watch how you say those holy words 'Oh my God'," admonished the semi-supreme being, "and be especially careful when and how you say *them*!"

"So then, if I had gone the alternate route and had married Carolyn," Richard introspectively reviewed, "I would be ahead of the game by at least two-hundred and forty-five thousand dollars between the farm market sale and the subsequent Ocean City, Maryland boardwalk arcade bonanza."

"But Carolyn would've been constantly unfaithful to you, and that kind of overwhelming grief cannot be measured in terms of dollars and cents," the majestically illuminated celestial guide advised. "Not everything Richard Henderson has a monetary value. But I must admit," the sagacious angel elucidated, "money is the root of all evil, second of course to having no money at all."

Next the helpful caring angel reminded Richard how *he* had gone into a second amusement arcade business with his former Ocean City, Maryland store managers in Atlantic City in 1977. But when the gambling industry entered the picture in the late seventies, the Missouri Avenue boardwalk lease was lost (by a small-print clause) to allow for the construction of the elaborate *Caesar's World Casino and Hotel*. The defunct Atlantic City, New Jersey venture had set the enterprising Richard Henderson back twenty-five thousand dollars.

"What a complete bummer!" Richard recalled and snottily answered. "You show motivation to work and a desire to get ahead, and then either the *IRS* or a stipulation in your greedy landlord's lease makes something valuable become absolutely worthless in a matter of seconds."

"Over the four year period Richard you lost over twenty-five thousand dollars," the angel reminded the then aspiring entrepreneur, "and your meager profits barely paying for two-thirds of the gaming equipment and pinball machines you had obtained to run the Atlantic City business. Mechanical poker machines are no match for electronic casino slot machines, that's for sure!" the angel deducted and opined. "I'm glad I was never a human, to tell you the honest-to-goodness truth. The pitfalls and dilemmas are entirely unbearable and just too pathetically numerous to endure!"

"And then my problems were compounded when I bought two one acre vacation lots I couldn't afford near Bushkill up in the *Pocono Mountains*," Henderson recollected and disclosed. "The Ocean City federal tax debacle, my strained marriage, along with the stupid Atlantic City and Bushkill ventures all proved to be enormous 'white elephants' in disguise. Bottomless money holes, that's all they were! And I had no lucrative cash cows to satisfy the debts of those all-too-deep money pits!" Richard convincingly elaborated to his receptive audience of one. "I still had to pay taxes on the empty Bushkill properties in addition to expensive community maintenance fees and ever-rising community association dues," Henderson informed (confessed to) the all-knowing angel. "I could never afford to build a house on either of those two very burdensome one-acre mountain lots, not with Jennifer Ranere as my un-supportive wife!"

The slightly sarcastic angel then proceeded to intensify Richard's aggravation by disclosing that if *he* had purchased the farm market, had married Carolyn, had sold the Ocean City arcade in 1975 then (with intelligent investing in utility stocks and safe mutual funds) he would now easily be a distinguished multimillionaire. "You would have wisely invested your ready cash in gold during the *OPEC* oil crisis in the seventies, and then your shrewd investment would've within two decades proliferated into a neat and tidy two million-dollar windfall."

"Now you tell me!" Richard replied and sneered. "Hindsight is always more accurate than foresight, that's for sure. And Carolyn would probably still have been unfaithful, even after I would've bought her mink coats, precious jewelry and a white *Mercedes*. But who would have cared? I would still have been rich enough to afford her lustful infidelity! I could've learned to live with Carolyn's unfaithfulness and with two million cold-cash dollars!"

"But you and Carolyn would never have had any children," the angel cautioned and maintained. "There is always a downside to any relationship, you know!"

"No children translates into having less headaches during a legal divorce," Richard ineffectively argued, "and besides, my three sons have all been brainwashed by their mother and by *her* greedy parents. 'Daddy's a no-body. Grand-pop gives us all *we* want. Daddy's unimportant in this family.' But I insist Angel that all I ever did was pay all the bills, that's all, while my wife Jennifer extravagantly spent, spent, spent!"

"Now you're being a little too cynical and self-defensive," the angel effectively reprimanded. "Humans all have their faults, you know, and unfortunately Richard, *that* rather simple principle also includes you."

"But I seemed to never learn a good lesson," Henderson confessed. "In 1981 I needed money so I ate humble pie and went back to the furniture store to give it another try. What a disaster that experiment turned out to be!"

"That's right," the supernatural guide amiably agreed. "Your father-in-law made you work like a donkey loading and unloading trucks filled with heavy sofas, dinettes, bureaus and beds. In the meantime *he* promoted and made your oldest son Jimmy your superior in the firm, telling you what to do and how to do it."

"Jimmy was a mischievous fifteen years old at the time," Richard remembered and sobbed, "and I was so infuriated and humiliated that I went and worked for a small rival furniture company located down the highway. I built that wimpy business up fifteen times its original size, but then..."

"But then the owner said that he didn't require your services any longer and terminated your commissioned employment. You were motivated by spite to make Mr. Ranere's competitor succeed," the angel accused. "You wanted to show your covetous father-in-law that *you* were competent enough to build up a nothing business into an awesome rival concern, a definite competitive threat to Mr. Ranere's financial base."

"Yes, but then my ecstasy was short-lived when old Mr. Jackson gave me the royal heave-ho. That is what you call gratitude for my invaluable contributions! An ugly pink slip!" Richard Henderson complained to his very wise listener. "Jackson gave me a swift kick in the butt when *he* should've sent praise and compensation my way! I was foolishly naïve to trust Jackson's promises on a handshake rather than specify the actual terms to our agreement in black and white on legal paper."

The all-intelligent angel presented a contrary point of view. He explained that Henderson had been able to sustain himself from the bonuses and commissions *he* had earned at the crafty competitor's furniture store. The heavenly visitor also reiterated how Richard had continued teaching and slowly was adding to his modest pension during those five years of employment in furnitureland, and how Richard had "miraculously" preserved his somewhat rocky marriage to Jennifer while winning the begrudging attention of his spiteful father-in-law.

"And so after all of these years of toil and calluses, all I got to show for it is a house with three unappreciative sons that have been spoiled rotten by their arrogant grandfather," the retired English teacher vehemently protested to the merciful and vaguely sympathetic angel. "What would have happened if I had married Carolyn? At least my head would've still been above water and I wouldn't have felt I needed to commit suicide in a desperate attempt to avoid bankruptcy and to escape reality!"

"Just the opposite," the angelic being confided as he waved his hand erasing the two rival furniture stores and then forming an authentic-looking power struggle inside of a judge's chamber with two smiling lawyers sitting at different sides of a very long formal-looking oak table. "Carolyn found and latched onto a wealthy corporate tycoon, a top executive in the computer industry," the angel informed his livid jittery companion. "But that arrangement didn't stop her from getting a four-hundred-thousand dollar settlement from you, basically your life's savings Richard. And then," the heavenly guide continued, "the stalking *IRS* finally caught up to you to tax your capital gains from your gold stock sales during the *OPEC* generated oil crisis. You had slyly figured that since you didn't receive any dividends or interest payments on your gold stock investments, the government computers would never catch up with your fantastic return on investment. But they eventually did! Yes Richard, they certainly did!"

"Well, that means I would've been no better off whether I had married Carolyn instead of getting hitched to Jennifer!" Richard Henderson exclaimed in utter astonishment. "Either way, my life was nothing more than one continuous gigantic misadventure! At least now Angel I know what would've happened if I had chosen different options."

"True to a certain extent," the affable and obliging angel concurred. "But there is one final hypothetical irony to this crazy parallel girlfriend dilemma that must be disclosed from your distant past. After Carolyn soaks you for your life's labor in the second parallel scenario," the angel divulged, "you go absolutely bonkers. You borrow heavily on your credit cards and invest in ten novels you've industriously spent the last twenty-five years writing and refining. You must be the ultimate idiot in the whole human race! That's what eventually pushed you to the threshold of bankruptcy in both marital scenarios!"

"I see," Richard softly answered in a defeated tone of voice. "I finally *see the light*, if you'll pardon the pun. I would be in the exact same monetary abyss regardless of whether I had married Carolyn and not had any children or had married Jennifer and had three not-so-wonderful sons. Either way my life would've been fraught with failure, misery and discontent. I'm basically a born loser, and that's essentially the long of it and the short of it!"

"It seems like you're magnetized to attract harassment and to lure mortification resulting from constant failure," the angel merrily chuckled to the not-too-thrilled loser. "So now that you know what would've happened to you if you had chosen the other forks in the road, would you now care to re-enter your former body and continue-on with your life?" the celestial messenger asked. "I have three other jobs I must perform this earthly day, so I hereby strongly request that you provide me with an immediate logical and rational response to my offered proposition."

Richard Henderson seriously weighed his winged colleague's proposal. The retired teacher considered how *he* had invested a thirty thousand dollar inheritance in the late 1980s' and how he had recklessly squandered it for the sake of an upstart computer company that contended it had a black box that could integrate and interpret all computer languages. 'A fool and his money are soon parted!' Henderson laughed to express his genuine reaction to an impromptu self-satire. 'And I really don't know whether I'm now heading to heaven, to hell or to purgatory!' the deceased fellow considered.

"Well, I'm waiting!" the angel insisted and demanded. "I'll give you only one minute more to decide."

"Let Carolyn be married to that fat-cat hotshot corporate computer honcho and let her reside in her opulent suburban mansion," Richard firmly uttered like an obsessed madman, "and let Jennifer and my three defiant sons exploit my friendly masochistic nature. I want to return to life on earth and enjoy every penny of my miserable thirty-thousand dollar a year pension and then gratefully enjoy the pleasure of anxiously awaiting the arrival of those hefty monthly social security checks starting next year," Henderson snickered to his newfound supernatural comrade.

"Then you mean you plan to return to life in Hammonton, New Jersey on the morning of April 24, 2002," the heavenly dispatched angel reaffirmed.

"Yes, that is my will!" the relieved and elated human verified rather enthusiastically.

"We have a pulse! We have a pulse!" the head paramedic of the Hammonton Rescue Squad shouted. "Let's stabilize this lucky soul and then get him into the ambulance. Notify the Emergency Room at Kessler Hospital that we're sending a rewired *flat-liner* over. This incredible man is nothing short of a major miracle! He must have a powerful guardian angel looking over him!"

Three weeks recovering in Kessler Memorial Hospital's *Intensive Care Unit* enabled Richard Henderson's condition to be up-graded from "life-threatening" to "critical," and after another week of hospitalization had elapsed the rejuvenated man was finally classified as "in stable condition" ready for immediate discharge upon doctor's approval.

After spending a month at home roaming the confined areas between his bed, his bathroom and his comfortable recliner chair, Richard Henderson finally summoned enough gumption, courage and stamina to shuffle down the upstairs' hallway to his son Jimmy's old bedroom. The faded gaudy wallpaper had been torn down and the walls had been spackled and then resurfaced with a tan coating of paint. The bedroom had been converted into "the computer room" right after the Henderson's oldest son sought independence of parental supervision and had moved out of the residence to live in his own condominium.

Reluctantly, Richard Henderson slowly entered his cherished captain's swivel chair and anxiously pressed the button in the center of his computer tower. His effort activated the system's monitor and the operator awaited the appearance of his *Internet* service provider's icon along with the other accompanying symbols on the start-up screen.

"Wouldn't it be great if I've sold another two dozen books between the time of my near death experience and my discharge from my extended hospital stay," Richard Henderson wishfully said to the inanimate screen situated before his eyes, the device stationed on top of his office's ancient-looking cherry wood desk. "I'm still surprised that two dozen strangers had taken the time and the energy to individually buy twenty-four of my idiotic novels in the first place. I guess I'm not a total failure!"

Richard's modem dialed into the *Internet* and he immediately visited the *Yahoo* search engine screen. He typed in his pen name and waited for the appropriate information to appear. The man scrolled down the list of items under "R.H. Factor" and was amazed. One hundred and twenty items were neatly catalogued,

130

and the first listing at the top of the web page conspicuously read "R.H. Factor at *Amazon.co.uk.*"

Henderson hastily traveled to *Amazon.co.uk* and was shocked to see all ten of his books listed in "Best Selling Order." He anxiously clicked on the first title, which showed it had an *Amazon.co.uk* sales ranking of 2,570. All of his other nine titles had impressive sales rankings ranging from ten thousand to one hundred thousand among from over three million online products.

Richard Henderson's heart was beating rapidly as he visited *Amazon.com, Amazon Germany, Amazon Japan, Amazon France, Barnes and Noble.com* and *Mobipocket.com* and the jubilant researcher quickly came up with similar high rankings for all ten of his creative novels.

The author sat dumbfounded before his computer screen, incredulously analyzing the inexplicable turn of events. After decades of futility, travail, hardship, disappointment, failure, rejection and an attempted suicide, fame and fortune had at last been accomplished. The man simply passively sat there and emotionally savored the sweet taste of success.

"I'm rich and famous thanks to my Guardian Angel's intervention into my death," Henderson mumbled to his image in a 1940ish wall mirror hanging above the five-year-old computer monitor. "It pays to follow your own instincts and not rely on anyone else to make *you* a success."

Footsteps were heard clambering up the colonial-style home's steps. The bedroom door flung open and young Jimmy Henderson was somewhat startled to see his father sitting before the computer in *his* old bedroom.

"Oh, hi Pop," the oldest son hesitantly greeted. "Hope you're feeling better this morning," Jimmy insincerely stated. "I just came by to get a few compact music discs I had left on the shelf in the closet before I moved out."

"Go right ahead son," Richard Henderson urged. "Take your time. When you get to be my age, you tend to value and relish every precious second."

"Pop, why do you waste your time on that dumb computer?" Jimmy disrespectfully criticized. "Grand-pop Jim is right. You'll never sell more than two dozen books for as long as you live. Grand-pop Jim says you're a born loser!" Jimmy Henderson sarcastically stated.

"I guess *you* and Grand-pop Jim have everything about my dismal life figured out," Richard Henderson coyly answered. "I wish I were only half as smart as either one of you two brilliant genetic geniuses!"

"The Rip Van Winkle Club"

William R. Stuyvesant unhappily lived with his domineering wife Gertrude in a magnificent Tarrytown, New York manor house situated on a palisade overlooking the majestic *Hudson River*. William often confidentially compared Gertrude (to male associates) to Dame Van Winkle, Rip Van Winkle's shrew of a wife who lambasted, browbeat and belittled the poor lethargic farmer every day from dawn until midnight. That is where the comparison between Gertrude Stuyvesant and Dame Van Winkle ends. William R. Stuyvesant was filthy rich and neither he nor Gertrude had to work another day in their lives to maintain their expensive tastes, hobbies and lifestyles.

William Stuyvesant, just like legendary Rip Van Winkle, claimed that Peter Stuyvesant, an early Dutch governor of New Netherland (later New Amsterdam, and now New York) was one of his paternal ancestors. William had inherited a considerable fortune from his father, a shrewd shopping center and real estate developer in the New York City metropolitan area. The fortunate beneficiary was lucky enough to parlay most of his inheritance in the stock market's high technology "bull rally" in the 1990s into a fantastic financial bonanza. But William's prosperity, his mansion and the spectacular view of the *Hudson River* constituted meager consolation when equated with Gertrude Stuyvesant's petulant hostile disposition. William believed that he was on the brink of a nervous breakdown.

"Gertrude is much-too-demanding. She's never happy until she's made me feel inferior by nagging, embarrassing and berating me day and night, oftentimes in front of others," William divulged to Harry Jenkins, one of his business partners over the telephone. "And while she's been spending time out in Los Angeles shopping like there's no tomorrow on *Rodeo Drive*, I've taken the liberty of purchasing a nice home up above Hudson on the river. It's a little more than an hour's drive from Tarrytown Harry, and I plan to use my new dwelling as a retreat for myself and some new friends I intend to make."

"Oh really," William's partner and business consultant doubtfully said, "and how do you intend to acquire these new friends? Make sure you don't get involved with riff-raff and swindlers! They're a dime a dozen nowadays. You might be putting your reputation in jeopardy so my advice is to be careful!" Harry Jenkins warned.

"Don't worry!" William R. Stuyvesant assured his apprehensive business contact. "Harry, I'll think of something to sift out the dirt from the gold."

William Stuyvesant was quite familiar with the stellar works of author Washington Irving and had often visited the literary giant's unique mansion *Sunnyside* located just below Tarrytown on the *Hudson's* eastern bank. The remarkable home, positioned just south of the *Tappan Zee Bridge* has been converted into a museum and is now open to the general public. Along with being an authority on Washington Irving's (1783-1859) mansion as well as on *his* biography, the multimillionaire also memorized virtually every passage in the author's works *The Alhambra, Knickerbocker's History of New York* and finally *The Sketch Book'*, which contained Irving's most popular tales, *The Legend of Sleepy Hollow* and *Rip Van Winkle.*

"You really love the *Catskill Mountains*, don't you Bill?" the building partner asked Stuyvesant over the phone. "My wife and I go up there all the time and stay at several plush resorts that we frequent. The *Catskills* are a great getaway in either summer or winter. We used to faithfully go to Grossingers and now we vacation at Villa Roma."

"Sure do love the *Catskills*," Stuyvesant acknowledged and agreed, "and next to Ichabod Crane, Rip Van Winkle has to be my favorite Washington Irving character. I think it all started when I read as a young boy about Rip Van Winkle leaving his village with his faithful dog Wolf to escape the tirades of wicked Dame Van Winkle. The poor henpecked fellow ascended *Thunder Mountain (Mt. Dunderberg)* to seek peaceful sanctuary from his scornful wife."

"Is that why you've bought that place up above Hudson on the river?" the voice on the other end of the telephone line asked. "Do you compare in your mind Gertrude Stuyvesant with Dame Van Winkle?" Harry Jenkins mildly interrogated. "You better not let Gertrude find that little secret out. She'll have you wallowing in bankruptcy in no time."

"Yes Harry, as a matter of fact I believe I did buy that property for that particular reason," Will Stuyvesant readily admitted. "Gertrude's temper tantrums are probably even worse than any that old Rip had to contend with from *his* overbearing Dame Van Winkle. I hope to find refuge and asylum from my matrimonial misery, and I want to bond and commiserate with other wealthy men that have egomaniac-type wives out to fleece their husbands of their hard-earned fortunes. Say Harry," William paused and then continued, "do you know what term Washington Irving coined for public consumption?"

"No, I haven't the slightest idea! What?" Harry's voice politely asked.

"The almighty dollar! Ha, ha, ha!" William Stuyvesant loudly laughed over the phone. "Those other rich fellows are guaranteed to empathize with my plight because they'll be in the exact same predicament as I am: rich, despondent, abused and perpetually badgered!"

"Okay Willy, good luck," Harry Jenkins offered. "Let me know how your social experiment works out with your new friends. Gotta' go!" Click.

'Poor Rip Van Winkle had the right idea,' William pensively thought while rubbing his chin. 'Even though *he* was poor, the *poor* fool needed to escape constant verbal abuse. I can send Gertrude to California and around the world, and despite my great fortune,' Stuyvesant imagined, 'the witch of a woman still berates and haunts me over the telephone. I definitely need isolation from her relentless antagonism. Yesterday the witch called me from Palm Springs and was shopping up a storm on Palm Canyon Drive. Tomorrow she'll be ten miles south in Palm Desert and hitting all of the ritzy stores on El Paseo!'

Then William R. Stuyvesant's mind was struck by a sudden inspiration. 'That's what I'll do,' he instantly decided. 'I'll run an ad in the business sections of *The New York Times* and *The Wall Street Journal.* I just want to see what kind of tangible results my lure will yield.'

The unhappy tycoon sat at his computer desk, went to his Microsoft Windows program and composed the following quarter of a page advertisement:

ATTENTION

Eligibility for admission to the prestigious *Rip Van Winkle Club* is now open. Candidates

must be of Dutch heritage, must have a
domineering, demanding and out-of-control
wife, and must also show proof of annual net
income of over a half million dollars. Benefits
include male bonding and many lucrative
business investment opportunities.   All
interested parties should submit documentation
(*IRS* annual tax statement and a bona fide copy
of birth certificate) to:

William R. Stuyvesant
P. O. Box 1783
Tarrytown, New York 10591

A full week passed without any meaningful responses to William Stuyvesant's unusual solicitation for qualified men to join the newly formed *Rip Van Winkle Club*. After ten days had elapsed from the publication of the *New York Times* and *Wall Street Journal* ads, the disappointed real estate developer thought that his "different idea" to form a social club of disparate and desperate wealthy male Dutch socialites had been both frivolous and futile. 'Perhaps I was a little too optimistic and naïve?' the multimillionaire thought.

But on the thirteenth day, applications began arriving at P.O. Box 1783, Tarrytown, New York, 10591. Twenty-four interested men sent in letters of introduction along with duplicate annual tax returns to validate minimum $500,000.00 net income along with accompanying copies of birth certificates to confirm authentic Dutch ancestry and heritage.

William was elated by the favorable response. He immediately hired the services of a reputable private detective agency to investigate into the backgrounds and careers of all two-dozen applicants. After finding fault with half of the male applicants for either being a joint partner in the half million dollar net income specification or for having only one parent of pure Dutch ancestry, the final list had diminished down to the following twelve lucky individuals:

Arnold Tromp	Stockbroker, Company Vice President
Hans Duncan	Appliance and TV Chain Store Owner
Charles Andersen	Insurance Adjuster, Business Owner

Salavatore Von Velardi	Executive, Import-Export Firm
Andrew Kondrack	Builder/Contractor
Peter Van Brocklin	Law Firm Senior Partner
Jack Zeeman	Dentist, Investor
James Erickson	Author of Bestsellers, Professor
Jesse Frank	Medical Doctor
Richard DeVries	Newspaper Publisher
Anthony Bosche	Accountant, *Fortune 500* Companies
Sam Vander Waals	Owner: Three Automobile Dealerships

'What an excellent list of fine entrepreneurial Dutch businessmen!' William thought and relished as he evaluated his final roster of names that had qualified for the newly amalgamated *Rip Van Winkle Club*. 'It's a wonderful cross-section of American free enterprise where honorable men of Dutch ancestry will exchange stock tips and share business investment opportunities while commiserating with one another the common bond of being continually badgered by bossy and dominant wives,' Stuyvesant thought and smiled. 'Gertrude's jet won't be flying home from *L.A.* until Sunday night. I'll have just enough time to schedule a cordial *Rip Van Winkle Club* get-together at my place for next Saturday afternoon. Then after we get acquainted, we'll have a small motorcade up to Hudson on the river and I'll show my kindred friends the newly renovated *RVW* club lodge, which will be available to any troubled member whenever *his* obnoxious wife starts to officially agitate and aggravate him.'

At six p.m. on Saturday the newly selected members of the *Rip Van Winkle Club* assembled at the Tarrytown palisades castle of William R. Stuyvesant. It was an interesting mix of personalities, but everyone shared one common denominator: *his* wife was a shrew' who would incessantly browbeat her successful husband into "chopped liver."

"Will, are you sure thirteen is a lucky number?" joked Andrew Kondrack, the real estate developer's new acquaintance. "I always had a weird phobia about the number thirteen! Not that I'm basically superstitious or anything."

"Thirteen sure *is* lucky, Andy," William answered after closely studying the building contractor's nametag. "Just remember Mr. Andrew Kondrack how lucky the original thirteen colonies were.

Thirteen might actually be the luckiest number in the universe for all we know!"

Everyone overhearing their' genial host's remark laughed heartily after its utterance. Instant camaraderie abounded, and soon the phenomenon known as "male bonding" set in as the thirteen new *Rip Van Winkle Club* friends having common Dutch genealogies, incomes and interests discussed random subjects like polo, golf, tennis, business, but most importantly, their despicable leeching wives.

"My old lady Helen makes Dame Van Winkle look like a novitiate nun," Richard DeVries, the flamboyant and effervescent newspaper mogul indicated to William and to Andrew Kondrack. "She's enough to make the Devil wish he was a blessed celibate saint! Helen's tongue must weigh more than three pounds, no exaggeration!"

"My spouse is so nasty that our neighbor's three Doberman pinscher attack dogs are super afraid of her!" an eavesdropping Hans Duncan added to the conviviality. "She makes *mean* seem like *kind*! Once during *Halloween* trick or treat night my wife scared two adults dressed like Dracula and Frankenstein right out of our neighborhood, and that's no hyperbole, either!"

"Will," Salvatore Von Velardi butted in as things quieted down around the bar, "when are we heading up to the *Catskills?* I need a little mountaintop rest and relaxation right this minute so I hope we don't accidentally wind-up in the *Adirondacks*. I can't wait to see your glorious lodge up above Hudson! And judging by the elegance of this mansion Will', I'll bet your little hideaway is pretty damned spectacular."

"After the third round of drinks have been imbibed," Will Stuyvesant promised his new friends, "we'll then all be on the same attitude adjustment wavelength and ready to begin *our* much-needed northern expedition. I'll lead the caravan with my sports utility vehicle," Will cheerfully volunteered and pontificated, "and I noticed that three of you men have 4-Wheel-Drive *SUVs* too. Use your four-wheel drive shift when we leave the paved road and have to climb up some steep terrain to arrive at my rustic sanctuary, or should I say *our* rustic sanctuary," Stuyvesant corrected himself. "It's thoroughly removed from all semblances of the hectic big city concrete jungle civilization!"

The men all boisterously cheered William R. Stuyvesant's exaggerated bravado, and after the third round of mixed drinks

138

had been swiftly gulped down by the jolly millionaires (assembled around the mansion's mahogany bar), the entourage was ready to embark on the first unprecedented weekend adventure of the newly formed *Rip Van Winkle Club.*

Soon the contingent of amiable half-intoxicated men left William's palatial residence and clambered into their respective vehicles. Four *SUVs* formed an impromptu mini-vacation caravan and William R. Stuyvesant led the jovial members in a military-type convoy north on *Highway 9,* which parallels the noble and serene *Hudson River.*

The small *SUV* fleet soon zoomed by *Sleepy Hollow High School* on the right-hand-side and shortly later down the busy road the autos' passed by Ossining, the infamous home of *Sing Sing State Prison.* Buildings belonging to *West Point Military Academy* were soon seen on the opposite shore of the stately river, and as the cavalcade of *SUVs* meandered around rocky embankments northward in the direction of downtown Poughkeepsie, the highway inclines became steeper and the picturesque landscape more rugged. All of the natural beauty brought out the "pioneering instinct" of the men sitting in William Stuyvesant's vehicle.

"Ah, communion with nature!" Will' said to Jack Zeeman, his loquacious and very grateful front seat passenger. "*Henry David Thoreau* would certainly enjoy this impressive mountain excursion we're now conducting. Too bad the loner was a poor guy and would be ineligible for membership into our club if that *Walden Pond* fellow were still alive."

"Yes, I'm sure *he* would *Thoreauly* be thrilled by it!" Jack Zeeman imaginatively returned. "We'll certainly enjoy some Transcendentalism without old Henry."

"Then Jack, you prefer this *Catskills'* outing to listening to your tempestuous wife ranting and raving all the time?" Will' deliberately inquired to get a reaction out of Zeeman. "We'll have to have a contest to see whose wife is more vicious! But I must admit that yours sounds hard to beat."

"The Rip Van Winkle Club sure beats Martha chewing me out about returning home late from night *Yankees* baseball games," Jack Zeeman merrily replied. "Martha's *barbs* are more painful than barbed wire!"

Backseat riders Charles Andersen and Jesse Frank found Jack Zeeman's marital impressions extremely hilarious as they boisterously laughed in response to the all-too-true declaration by the henpecked dentist' "riding shotgun" up front with Will Stuyvesant.

"Maybe your wife scolds you because she's an avid *Mets'* fan!" Jesse Frank amusingly suggested to Jack Zeeman. "There might be some hidden baseball vindictiveness there! Maybe Jack, Martha owns stock in the *Mets'* without you even knowing about it. Ha, ha, ha!"

"Or maybe Martha is hard of hearing," offered Charlie Andersen, "because I know for a fact that people' with severe hearing problems tend to yell when speaking to others so that they can then hear themselves talking! And that's no joking either! I'm bet Jack that your ferocious wife Martha has some sort of hearing disability. Ha, ha, ha!"

"I don't think so!" the blithe-spirited Jack Zeeman chortled from the front seat. "If George Washington's Martha was anything like Martha Zeeman is, then the great *Revolutionary War* General would have become a *Tory* and jumped over to the *British* side just to get away from his wife's flagrant diatribe. Old George would've been a turncoat for the redcoats!"

"If that's the case," William laughed as he rounded a sharp curve in the road, "then Benedict Arnold must've had an overbearing savage wife very similar to your Martha!" Stuyvesant gleefully exclaimed to Jack Zeeman. Wild cackling and guffawing coming from the back seat resulted from Stuyvesant's sarcastic but acutely humorous comment.

The short procession of *SUVs* proceeded with *their* small expedition up *Route 9* and at late twilight passed through Hyde Park, rapidly buzzing by the historic and picturesque home of the revered Franklin Delano Roosevelt, the mansion/museum now converted into a popular national shrine. After driving past the magnificent Hudson River *Vanderbilt Mansion* on the left, the four-vehicle caravan continued on its itinerary heading north, the drivers' next destination being Rhinebeck, a town rich in tradition dating back to the colonial era.

"I understand that George Washington once slept at the *Rhinebeck Inn,*" William informed his still giddy and amused passengers, "and it's really a pretty neat place to spend the night, even with *your* wife Jack! Maybe Gorge Washington's Martha is still in there," William joked to Jack Zeeman, much to everyone's delight.

"If Washington slept at all these places that claim he had slumbered in their beds," Charles Andersen cynically volleyed from the rear, "then Washington would've slept his way right through the entire *Revolutionary War* just like poor exploited Rip Van Winkle had done."

"I guess that the signers of the *Declaration of Independence* put their money on Washington to be our nation's top general because they figured he'd be a real *sleeper!*" Jesse Frank obnoxiously hollered and punned from the backseat.

"You guys are really a lot of fun!" William admitted as he stopped for a red traffic signal. 'I'm glad you all decided to get away from your nasty marital mates and get together for leisurely weekends up at my place in the *Catskills*. So far, you fellas' have been a real pleasure to be with," Stuyvesant commended his jolly passengers. "We all need to unwind from our daily stressful schedules and also need to evade our wicked wives' negative bullying and intimidation."

Finally the four vehicles followed *Route 9* into the town of Hudson, where the highway converted into Fairview Avenue', which the caravan stayed on until the appearance of Rod and Gun Road on the left. After several miles of asphalt surface, William held his hand out of the opened driver-side window, signaling to the three trailing *SUVs* to enter four-wheel drive and then take a stone and gravel road up to *his* mountain retreat lording over the dignified placid *Hudson River*.

"You know," William said to his alert and jovial companions in a philosophical tone of voice, "I can just picture poor Rip Van Winkle ascending these steep precipices on a cloudy fall day with his hunting dog Wolf just to achieve some much needed requiem from Dame Van Winkle's perpetual tyranny. We all know poor Rip Van Winkle's burden all-too-well from local folklore! In fact Washington Irving aptly described Rip's unenviable plight as petticoat tyranny! Ha, ha, ha!"

"Make sure our first toast at the lodge is dedicated to the fond memory of Rip Van Winkle," Jack Zeeman recommended to his merry colleagues. "All in favor say 'aye'!"

"Aye!" his three cohorts bellowed in raucous-but-sincere unanimity.

* * * * * * * * * * * *

The good-natured men spent the night engaged in serious entertainment and whimsical amusement. They played cards, chess, checkers and dominoes. They drank expensive whiskeys, imported beer and vintage wines. After eating a late catered supper featuring fried chicken, baked ham and basted turkey, the new fraternity members of the *Rip Van Winkle Club* reminisced about past steamy romances and about exotic tropical vacations in Hawaii, the Caribbean and along the French Riviera. Will was elated that the members were all compatible, sharing and building a newfound camaraderie.

Next the club members conversed about the simple joys identified with the biological processes known as eating and drinking, and finally the topic of conversation centered upon the very unfortunate marital predicament of the newly organized club's splendid namesake, Rip Van Winkle.

"Rip drank the delicious Holland gin obtained from an enchanted barrel at Henry Hudson's wild mountain party," Will' nostalgically recollected (and reminded his newfound friends) from the Washington Irving legend, "and the powerful substance put our favorite reveler to sleep for twenty long years. That's not such a bad sentence when you're married to an overbearing shrew like Dame Van Winkle, who sounds almost as treacherous as Jack Zeeman's wife Martha."

"That twenty year sleep was more of a blessing than a curse," Andrew Kondrack steadfastly maintained. "Old Rip didn't have to confront or listen to his belligerent wife's ugly outbursts for two whole decades."

"Yes, most definitely a truism," Peter Van Brocklin chimed in, "but poor Rip lost twenty valuable years off his life where he could've enjoyed many satisfying draughts of ale at Nicholas Vedder's tavern. The impoverished Dutch farmer returned to his village twenty years later not recognizing a single inhabitant in the entire place."

"I really feel badly for the exploited gent, even if he was only a fictitious character," Anthony Bosche amiably qualified and contributed to the discussion. "First of all, we all sleep eight hours a day, so that means we really only consciously live around fifty years instead of the customary seventy-five-year average that biology textbooks and encyclopedias inaccurately state. One third' of our lives is spent snoring in bed!"

142

"I see where you're getting at Tony," interrupted William R. Stuyvesant. "Rip Van Winkle was callously cheated another twenty years by Henry Hudson's cruel sleeping spell, so in effect, Rip was an old man at only thirty years of age. What a lousy bummer no matter how one studies it!"

After cleaning up the extensive waste the sumptuous feast had generated, the euphoric men strolled out to the four *SUVs* and removed their suitcases to lug into "the RVW Lodge." Soon the sportive gentlemen all retired to their assigned quarters, satisfied and content, waiting for a morning of adventure following a restful night's slumber.

The next morning, dark clouds shrouded the distant mountain peaks, making that particular extension of the great *Appalachian* chain appear clad in a dull blue and purple-hued haze. Peter Van Brocklin, Salvatore Von Velardi and Andrew Kondrack were early risers that could have taught the area Hudson roosters a lesson or two in "dawn punctuality." The three new acquaintances were casually standing on the back patio' deck of William R. Stuyvesant's "backwoods retreat" and were admiring the scenic tranquility of the passive *Hudson River* down in the valley while contemplating and discussing the awesome *Catskill Mountains*. William R. Stuyvesant exited the expansive converted ranch-home-to-lodge overlooking the *Hudson* and soon joined his guests. The sightseers were carrying three pair of binoculars with a fourth very expensive pair being strapped around Will's neck.

"Here, use these peepers to survey the pristine beauty that surrounds us!" Will' suggested as he handed his high-tech' high-powered binoculars to the three men casually stationed on the wooden platform deck. The four spectators took turns peering into the new ultra-modern magnifiers and with their elbows resting on a sturdy black wrought iron railing', the men gazed out at the wondrous environmental splendors all around them. Suddenly something highly irregular had been spotted.

"Hey guys," Andrew Kondrack observed and said in a mellow but serious tone of voice, "there seems to be some kind of ancient ship anchored out near that rock formation down there to our right. Can you guys see it?"

All four pair of binoculars instantly focused on Andrew Kondrack's curious sighting. William R. Stuyvesant, a student of

Dutch antiquity, immediately recognized the identity of the object in question.

"Well I'll be a chimpanzee's cousin!" Will' emphatically marveled and exclaimed. "That ship down there in the river is a replica of *Henry Hudson's* prized vessel, the *Half Moon*. Has anyone read any recent newspaper articles about a model of the *Half Moon* visiting this area of New York north of Hudson? That's what that ship has to be, a replica!"

None of the men recollected reading any such journalism, so Will anxiously suggested that the *Rip Van Winkle Club* membership hop into the four *SUVs* and take a narrow side trail down the scenic mountainside to investigate the strange ship anchored near the *Hudson's* shore.

The men inside the house were summoned from their shaving in front of vanity mirrors, from the breakfast table and from their beds, and in a matter of five hectic minutes, all thirteen adventurous souls scrambled outside the lodge and into the vehicles. Will' led the way in his silver *Ford Expedition* down the steep sloping trail to the vicinity where the mysterious ship had dropped anchor in the historic river.

Upon reaching a plateau overlooking the "facsimile *Half Moon*," the four *SUVs* halted one after the other in military parade fashion and the thirteen intrigued occupants got out in a hurry to satisfy their heightened curiosity about the handsome ship of yore and its crew. Much to their astonishment, three little men, each no more than four and a half foot tall, were climbing up an embankment and approaching the men's location from below.

Each of the tiny grizzled-bearded men was dressed in the antique Dutch fashion that was emblematic of late seventeenth century haberdashery. Their extraordinary attire was comprised of cloth' jerkins, and below the short coats the cute but sour-faced fellows wore several pairs of baggy breeches that were handsomely ornamented with rows of buttons lined down each side. Each diminutive "midget Dutchman" (as Will Stuyvesant had labeled them) had been toting on *his* shoulder a small barrel, more of a cask than a barrel, and each fellow appeared quite encumbered by *his* object's weight. The little gents seemed preoccupied with their strenuous labor and were unperturbed by the sudden appearance and confrontation of the thirteen tall men recently arrived from the Rip Van Winkle Lodge.

"Hey little guys," Will Stuyvesant affably greeted, "let us help you carry your barrels up the mountain. We're just brimming with energy."

"This must be some kind of re-enactment of the *Rip Van Winkle* tale," Salvatore Von Velardi conjectured and articulated to all within hearing distance. "But if this experience is true and not a mass hallucination, then these tiny men will lead us to Henry Hudson and his *Half Moon* crew."

Just then a loud rumble of thunder rolled through the distant mountains, and the noise was succeeded by additional low growling peals to the northwest.

"Legend says that that's Henry Hudson and his crew of little men playing a friendly game of ninepins up in the *Catskills*," Peter Van Brocklin related to anyone and everyone willing to listen. "If I'm not mistaken, these little men will take us to *their* leader just like they had done with Rip Van Winkle."

The thirteen visitors assisted the three wee individuals with *their* indigenous labor, thus alleviating much of *their* struggle and toil. About five hundred feet up a narrow rocky footpath, the head small Dutchman dressed in ancient garb uttered to a solid rock façade, "In Henry Hudson's great name, open a shortcut to *our* destination's game."

Amazingly, the dense rock façade slowly swung open as if it was a lightweight door on hinges. A long dark tunnel was immediately exposed and soon the sixteen human forms took turns lugging the three liquor casks further into the dark hollow, which extended a thousand feet or so into the base of the mountain ridge.

A dull light was visible at the tunnel's other end, and upon exiting the black cavity, the sixteen trekkers instantly perceived a beautiful ravine with rolling mounds and lush green grassy meadows. Luxurious sunshine radiated down on the splendid dell, and at least fifty other little men dressed in the same-style sixteenth century ancient Dutch costumes were idly standing around and engaging in small talk. But each tiny gent had a very melancholy expression on his face.

"Why are they all so sad looking?" Andrew Kondrack whispered to Will Stuyvesant after the two millionaires lowered their heavy cask onto a wooden platform that had been tacitly designated by one of the solemn tiny fellows. "To use one of Jack London's favorite words, they all look 'lugubrious'."

"According to legend," Will speculated and whispered, "these little men are immortal. They are unchanging in age as time advances onward. Because they're all immortal," Will Stuytvesant continued his explanation, "they're bored with their mortal existence and unhappy having to live forever. They've seen everything once too often and are not at all enamored with the monotony of life's repetitious events."

"And check out those mischievous little imps partying over there," Jack Zeeman indicated to his companions with his right hand. "They're playing a game of bowling on the green and simulating the sound of thunder echoing through the mountains when the ball strikes the pins."

"Ninepins, not bowling," Will' aptly corrected. "That game is often referred to as duckpins!"

Henry Hudson dispatched one of his chief wee English-speaking crewmembers to the area of the thirteen spellbound twenty-first century Americans, and after a polite introduction, Heinrick addressed his former helpers.

"Thank you for assisting us in transporting the Holland gin to our big party," Heinrick began his impromptu speech. "As you gentlemen might know every twenty years the crew of the *Half Moon* returns to the *Hudson River Valley* to review and celebrate our past explorations and expeditions. It's quite a treat for us despite our sad-looking countenances."

"Have you ever heard of a fellow named Rip Van Winkle?" Jack Zeeman asked Heinrick.

"That's confidential information I'm not at liberty to discuss," Heinrick diplomatically answered.

"Well then, how come there're three barrels of Holland gin and not just one?" Will' asked the peculiar-looking neurotic-sounding little fellow. "Are you intending to have a bigger party than usual this afternoon?"

"Well kind Sir," Heinrick defensively said, "I strongly suggest that you listen attentively. The gin from each of the barrels will produce a different effect. One barrel's contents will have no effect on the drinker of its gin, one of the barrels will age the drinker twenty years, and a chug from the third random barrel will make the lucky drinker twenty years younger."

"Wow!" Hans Duncan (the wealthy appliance distributor) amply exclaimed. "It's sort of like a casino gamble on the wheel game with numbers one to three rotating around," Hans

146

accurately interpreted. "If I choose correctly and can tack twenty years onto my life and simultaneously become two decades younger in the meantime," Hans hypothesized and declared, "then it's worth the gamble to be able to outlive my nasty wife."

"And even if *you* choose to drink from the wrong cask," Charlie Andersen guessed and explained, "then *you* still might choose the barrel that'll have no effect at all and still enjoy a cool refreshing mug of Holland gin. That's a fifty-fifty chance."

"But fellas'," Will Stuyvesant cautioned his newfound comrades, "if someone selects the wrong barrel out of the three, then that person will be doomed to losing twenty years off his already pathetic life and will wake up an old man ready for the cemetery. Is that gambol worth the gamble?"

"Do you mean to say that *you* believe all this idiotic nonsense?" Arnold Tromp criticized. "This is the most preposterous hoax I've ever witnessed. It *is* in my fairly astute estimation and educated opinion that this farce is absolutely beyond a shadow of a doubt a silly college fraternity-type initiation prank of the greatest magnitude!"

"Then you Sir wouldn't hesitate to prove *me* wrong by taking the first sample," Heinrick offered Arnold Tromp as the gallery of fifty little men in attendance laughed exceedingly at their foreman's intelligent challenge to *his* dubious guest. "Would you care to sample a sip Mr. Arnold Tromp?"

"Well, I'll have to think about it and reconsider my options," Arnold Tromp uneasily conceded. "This is indeed a most difficult choice we're being pressured into making. Hey! How did *you* know my name?"

Again, the fifty or so little men roared out in laughter as the sound of a small rolling ball smashed against a triangular formation of duckpins on the ravine's lush green.

"I'll bet a thousand dollars with any of you that this decision Henry Hudson is presenting us with is for real," William R. Stuyvesant boldly offered the other twelve astonished members of the *Rip Van Winkle Club*. "Who's got the guts to put *his* money where his mouth is?"

All of the twelve other "party crashers" presumed and believed that the entire scenario was a "clever theatrical trick" that had been brilliantly contrived, paid for, sponsored and orchestrated by their illustrious host, William R. Stuyvesant of Tarrytown, New York. Salvatore Von Velardi was the first bold fellow to bet a thousand dollars, believing that Will' would graciously reimburse him after the completion of "the chicanery." The other eleven meanderers all gave *their* pledge that they would pay William R. Stuyvesant a thousand dollars each should "the deception" indeed turn out to be a "functioning aberration."

William was nominated to choose first, so Stuyvesant drank a cup of Holland gin from barrel number three. Arnold Tromp, Salvatore Von Velardi, Peter Van Brocklin, James Erickson, Jesse Frank and Sam Vander Waals all were given empty mugs that were quickly filled and the "guinea pigs" heartily quaffed down their draughts drawn from barrel number two.

The remaining six thoroughly entertained wealthy gentlemen all lustily drank down Holland gin from the cask labeled in Dutch "Number One."

Will Stuyvesant began feeling dizzy, first losing his balance with wobbly knees and then acting irrational with planets, stars and galaxies spinning around inside his head. The intoxicated multimillionaire staggered and tottered about, clumsily and awkwardly gyrating from side to side as if he were a defective spinning top. The organizer of the *Rip Van Winkle Club's Catskill Mountain* excursion trudged off walking between and around several jagged crags, disappearing over the horizon as he cautiously attempted descending the rugged ridge while still under the influence of the very potent Holland gin.

Stuyvesant's twelve skeptical and traitorous apostles also staggered around like a bevy of soused alcoholics, desperately searching for a soft spot on the velvet-green-grass to take much-needed naps. Each man's fate was determined by the numbered cask from which *he* had selected a draught to drink.

Hans Duncan, Charles Andersen, Andrew Kondrack, Jack Zeeman, Richard DeVries and Anthony Boshe all unfortunately drank the Holland gin from barrel "Number One." Each man was destined to sleep in the mystical *Catskill Mountains* for twenty-years and thusly validating himself' as a true disciple of the inimitable Rip Van Winkle and also demonstrating that *he* was a dedicated member of the *Rip Van Winkle Club*. Upon waking up, Richard DeVries, the youngest of the first cask group would be age seventy-one in the year 2022, and Andrew Kondrack, the eldest among the ill-fated half dozen would be ninety-two upon awakening from his unanticipated slumber two decades later.

As for the imbibers that partook of the second cask, Arnold Tromp, Salvatore Von Velardi, Peter Van Brocklin, James Erickson, Jesse Frank and Sam Vander Waals all were miraculously rejuvenated with twenty years fantastically shaved off their ages. However, the sly and clever dwarf' Heinrick had not disclosed to the vain and gullible men that they would be assigned as cabin boys to perform myriad duties and drudgery-assignments on the good ship *Half Moon*. And regrettably, the six hapless victims of youth revisited were all now permanently destined to have futures laden with misery as servants of the no-nonsense taskmaster Henry Hudson and his disconsolate and temperamental crew of fickle little seventeenth century Dutch men.

As for William R. Stuyvesant, the foundering founder of the notorious *Rip Van Winkle Club*, his fate was not a benign one, either. The multimillionaire awoke (without any signs of aging) just before dawn on Sunday morning and found himself' lying on soggy turf between a termite-infested hollowed-out fallen oak tree and a clump of mountain sticker bushes and accompanying briers.

William immediately recollected his misadventure the day before with the mischievous little ghostly Dutchmen in the very outlandish *Catskill Mountain* amphitheater-like ravine. The victim felt arthritis in his wrists and elbows and rheumatism in his back's lumbar area. Will's initial instinct was to feel for a long, shaggy gray beard', which would be evidence that he had been betrayed by Henry Hudson and *his* naughty crew and that *he* had indeed slept for twenty years just like his legendary mentor, Rip Van Winkle. Stuyvesant was glad to note that no lengthy grizzled beard had grown from his face and the befuddled man was never so happy to feel his whiskers' bristles.

'I wonder what happened to the others?' William meditated as he feebly rose to his feet and then brushed some skittering insects and loose dirt from his light-blue denim jeans and from his navy blue sweatshirt. 'I hope I can find my way out of this forsaken place and back to my *SUV*. Thank God I had only slept for one night!'

The addled fellow's head was still groggy from the potent alcohol he had consumed the prior morning, so Will' prudently shuffled down the ridge and soon recognized the odd ravine where the games of ninepins had been played. 'This is also where

I had made the mistake of taking the first sample of Holland gin from the third cask,' he regretted with a degree of guilt. 'This is like a nightmare revisited.'

Being distracted by his own vain thoughts, William accidentally stumbled over a log, fell onto the ground and then tumbled forward several hundred feet down a slope to the footpath that led to the dark tunnel shortcut through the base of the mountain. 'I think I know where I'm at now!' he thought.

After Stuyvesant had rolled down to the base of the ravine, much to his consternation the tunnel exit was not observable, so Will' remembered the rhyming language uttered by diminutive Heinrick at the long hollow dank rock corridor's other end. "In Henry Hudson's great name, open a shortcut to *my* destination's game!" Stuyvesant shouted with his hands cupped over his mouth, his voice echoing throughout the ravine and resounding through the surrounding mountain precipices.

The rock façade slowly creaked open like a squeaky door with rusty hinges, revealing the same fabulous tunnel shortcut that the three dwarfs had led the loyal members of the *Rip Van Winkle Club* through the morning before. 'This tunnel is like a magical umbilical cord connecting the material world with a bizarre fantasy world,' Will's dazed mind thought and concluded. 'Now all I have to do is walk the thousand feet, get inside my *SUV* and drive back to civilization. I almost want to see and hear Gertrude again!' the explorer insanely imagined.

The secret tunnel was just as damp and dreary as it had been the day before, and upon entering the outside world dimmed by a dark cloudy overcast sky on the opposite end, the rock façade soon mechanically squealed shut much to Will Stuyvesant's awe and bewilderment. Then the solid rock door banged against the mountain base with a thud, quite effectively concealing its secret access to the secluded magical ravine.

Still stunned and mildly disoriented from his ordeal, William Stuyvesant cautiously descended the final three hundred feet down a ridge, the route leading to the aforementioned mountain trail where the four all-terrain vehicles had been neatly parked in a row the morning before. 'I must take it slow, for if I plunge down this last incline from this height,' Will assessed, 'then I'll risk breaking an arm, a leg or both. If I survive this ordeal no one's ever going to believe my tale! Hey, all four SUVs are still down there!'

With careful diligence, the man's aching legs finally carried his weary body down the remaining part of the ridge closest to his trusty four-wheel drive vehicle. The sky was still partially dark with the new day's sun ready to perform its daily resurrection on the black and pink eastern horizon.

Arriving at his *Ford Expedition*, Will frantically fumbled in his jeans' pockets for his keys but then he remembered that in his rush to make contact with Heinrick and *his* two dwarfish associates, Stuyvesant had inadvertently left the starting device in the *SUV's* ignition. 'Thank God it's still there,' Will thought as he opened the driver-side door and gingerly entered his beloved vehicle. 'Now to get out of here!'

The reliable *Expedition's* motor whined and then started and next Will' methodically backed the vehicle up and gingerly turned the *SUV* around with his hood pointed in the direction of downtown Hudson. 'I should report the whole insane incident to the police,' Stuyvesant logically considered, 'but the cops would never believe me in a million years. The only thing I have going for me is my credibility and my track record of being a multimillionaire and the fact that twelve highly successful businessmen will soon be reported missing to the authorities. I feel that I'm responsible for all of these bizarre things happening!'

William had an inclination to turn on the specially installed *Bose* radio system to listen to the news but before he could honor his next impulse, the man's eyes instantly beheld a dark foreboding spectral image remaining stationary three hundred feet ahead. An ominous frightening figure sitting atop an enormous black horse stood directly in *his* path.

'Oh my God!' Will's mind recognized and feared. 'It's the fabled *Headless Horseman of Sleepy Hollow*! How could a fictitious character from one legend suddenly enter into the enactment of another? This is too surreal to be real! Not even Gertrude would wish such a cursed torture on me!'

Will sat petrified like a contemporary Ichabod Crane in the front driver's seat of his dependable *Ford Expedition*, believing that *he* could outrace the formidable ruthless *Headless Horseman* once *he* could safely make it to a paved highway. The driver slowly inched forward, waiting for the right opportunity to gun the silver *SUV* onto a side gravel and stone' winding road that paralleled the majestic *Hudson River*.

Showing marvelous timing and dexterity, Stuyvesant quickly rotated the steering wheel to the right and soon his vehicle was speeding down the mountain ridge trail with the swift black horse and its tenacious executioner closing the gap between Stuyvesant and the rider's speedy stallion. Stuyvesant had never been so alarmed and so panic-stricken in all his life.

Will's speedometer registered fifty miles an hour as he maneuvered around precarious curves and up and down treacherous terrain that would not ordinarily accommodate such high speed, but much to *his* trepidation, the well-conditioned horse remained close behind. Fortunately a mile stretch of straightaway was dead ahead for Will', so Stuyvesant again mashed his foot down on the accelerator, with the dependable *SUV* rapidly attaining a speed of eighty miles per hour. Still, the fleet galloping black steed was easily able to keep pace with the great instant velocity achieved by the silver *Ford Expedition*.

'This is impossible!' Will' thought. 'Not even a gazelle or a cheetah could run this fast! This is contrary to reason! It goes against both nature and science!'

The fantastic wildly snorting black steed with its determined headless rider in the saddle then incredibly pulled alongside the terrified *SUV* driver. A totally hysterical and delirious Will Stuyvesant took a brief glimpse at the shocking apparition', which suddenly removed a handgun from a concealed pocket inside its ghostly apparel and then aimed and fired the weapon at the *SUV's* front wheel.

The bullets from the devastating blasts punctured the *Expedition's* left front tire. Will Stuyvesant abruptly lost control of the speeding all-terrain vehicle. The SUV veered to the right off of the already dangerous stone and gravel road, careened down a ridge of smooth weather-worn rocks and then violently plummeted into the tranquil *Hudson River*. Both William Reynolds Stuyvesant's life and the short-lived *Rip Van Winkle Club* had been fatefully and simultaneously erased from the face of the earth.

Much to the shock of Hudson River Valley aristocrats, after *his* corpse had been recovered from the river, Will Stuyvesant's obituary appeared three days later in New York City and Tarrytown newspapers. Accolades abounded in the print media articles. Stuyvesant was described and praised as a "generous community minded philanthropist" who will be deeply missed by

his affectionate wife Gertrude Stuyvesant, who later tearfully
eulogized her husband during his church funeral services and
then thereafter cried incessantly at his solemn burial.

About the Author

Jay Dubya is author John Wiessner's pen name and also his initials (J.W.). John is a retired New Jersey public school teacher, having diligently taught the subject for thirty-four years. John lives in Hammonton, New Jersey with wife Joanne, and the couple has three grown sons.

John has written and e-published twenty-six books. Besides *Pieces of Eight, Part III*, he has authored its companion books, *Pieces of Eight, Pieces of Eight, Part II* and *Pieces of Eight, Part IV*. All four works contain short stories and novellas that feature science fiction and paranormal plots and themes. *Nine New Novellas*, *Nine New Novellas II*, *Nine New Novellas III* and *Nine New Novellas IV* are short story collections that parallel those in the *Pieces of Eight* series.

Other Jay Dubya adult-oriented fiction are the works *Black Leather and Blue Denim, A '50s Novel*, and its exciting sequel, *The Great Teen Fruit War, A 1960' Novel*. *Frat Brats, A '60s Novel* completes the "coming of age" trilogy. Jay Dubya also has produced two irreverent Biblical satires, *The Wholly Book of Genesis* and *The Wholly Book of Exodus*. A third satire *Ron Coyote, Man of La Mangia* is also a parody on Miguel Cervantes' classic novel, *Don Quixote* published in 1605. Other satirical works are *Mauled Maimed Mangled Mutilated Mythology* and *Fractured Frazzled Folk Fables and Fairy Farces* (*I and II*). *Thirteen Sick Tasteless Classics*, *Thirteen Sick Tasteless Classics II*, *Thirteen Sick Tasteless Classics III* and *Thirteen Sick Tasteless Classics IV* are other humorous parody works.

The author has also penned a young adult fantasy trilogy, *Pot of Gold, Enchanta* and *Space Bugs, Earth Invasion*. *The Eighteen Story Gingerbread House* is another children's literature work.

Jay Dubya really likes '50s music and he also listens to songs by the Beatles, *ELO*, the Carpenters, the Beach Boys, Fleetwood Mac, the Eagles, the Rolling Stones, John Mellencamp and by John Fogerty.

When not listening to popular music, Jay Dubya prefers watching *76ers'* basketball and *Phillies* and *Yankees'* television baseball games.